Worm Children:

Children of the Same Crop

Gruber Van Fiether

D1525662

Copyright

Contents

DISCLAIMER: Any likeness to any real persons, groups, or ideas, or to any fictional characters, places, or concepts not of my design, is entirely coincidental.

FOREWORD

Recognize that every dunder-head to denounce my so-called "imperfections" and "incongruities" succumbs to the superiority of my further evolved mind. Indeed, skeptics have merely failed to escape my predatory jaws of language; they–the critics, the naysayers, the plebeian opposition–they lack a certain enhanced level of visionary cognition, combined perfectly with a moderate dose of what conventional society brands "insanity," to correctly perceive as deliberate genius what a simpleton may deduce to be carelessness or inaccuracy. Find your niche on the scale of mental evolution, but do not be discouraged by its futile rank.

Only by chance are these first words still soaking in the ink in which I have scribbled them, even after I withdrew my pen from the last stroke of the final letter. By some odd feat had I written this book by the lamplight of my own room as the sun retired, and yet I neatly stack these papers, lined in writing, awaiting their first embrace by the gentle Dawn, in the shade of the early morning. Words poured from my pen continuously; the only limiting factor to the completion of this manuscript was the time ink takes to dry.

Delicious were the wanderings of my conscience. Yes, forever will my heart reside in this warm cauldron. For a night, I have immersed myself in a figment realm; I have disappeared from my desk and strolled the boulevards of a world over the ocean of my own mind. I walk and dream. Feel me follow as you read, and feel the others as well. They know who we are. I understand someone witnesses my transgressions here as I selfishly steal the secrets of this place, for it would be privilege enough to observe quietly and confide these accounts in my own record. My eye gazes outward through this branch I sprout—a branch that reaches out, thirsting. Accompanying the moon, I retire from my writing indefinitely, and the last limb of my imagination dances with the music of the following words:

PROLOGUE

"Welcome to the Zero Zone; Population: Unknown" the sign ambiguously declares. As I leap into the void and the dimensional membrane shatters, the universal consciousness immediately digests my own. I assimilate into omniscience; all wisdom that has ever been known overwhelms me in an intellectual flood. A species of cerebral equilibrium develops in which my intelligence circulates into and magnifies the Omnicogna, while it concurrently returns equivalent information into me. Eventually, of course, the equipoise dissolves, for while the infinite expertise of The Mind continues to cascade into my own, I am incapable of offering it further education, rudely obliterating the temporary symmetry. The inundation of sudden enlightenment sparks celestial flares, striking hotly upon the ever exploding surface of my endogenous being. In processing such discharge of immeasurable insight, a cosmic frequency hums a single discordant blur of obtrusive sapience, and the tintinnabulation rattles like an unfathomable shock. Yet somehow through the chaotic dissension of this silent, interstellar screech, I comprehend the pattern in everything and within all (spirals in circles and cycles in orbit). The immaculate disorder evokes natural peace in the most spiritually beautiful sense.

I conclude with increasing clarity that this dimension, this so-called "Zero Zone," embodies the very essence of strangeness and indescribability, for while it exists merely theoretically as a tear in the space-time continuum, a vacant wasteland toward which all thought gravitates, it is in fact the only habitat in which everyone has presence and all collective knowledge can be accumulated and partitioned. The very concept of the Zero Zone confuses and

7

frightens me with its foreign mechanisms, but, contradictingly, I feel composed and at-home, genuinely familiar with my surroundings as if I'd previously frequented this hub of subconsciousness. Here, not even the Puppeteer himself has potence; his strings tug on emptiness and Zero, groping and squirming through space, fingering blackness for anything at all. This is, indeed, a curious place.

The Keeper of Secrets beckons me with specific instructions, and though I am fully aware of his inexistence, his commanding authority intimidates me into obedience. Acquiescing to his implicit demands, I sift through the factual catalogue with an egotistical sieve, plucking bits of data pertinent to my life. Good Keeper, I think, thank you for the enlightenment that upon me you bestow. Benevolent Oświec, Guardian of the Mind, Slayer of Ignorance, Collector of Wisdom, my utmost gratitude is yours, for my blindness liquefies at your whim. My sophistication resumes.

Particles manifest and arrange themselves in various configurations, unanimously settling in the form of a wee infant. I make no mistake in identifying the suckling as myself, moments after birth, and upon a proficient swipe of the Keeper's zero-dimensional staff, every moment of my life simultaneously presents itself to me. I spontaneously absorb all information, and my memory stretches to its breaking point as I recognize each event with enlightened perception. Ah, what artistry is the endeavor of life! What allure accompanies each slice of time as it materializes in its own interdimensional fissure! How I yearn to relive each juncture, to enhance each accomplishment. Life's blunders are far too swift to anticipate and are suffered regardless of preparation. But I found myself always instinctively able to parry any of life's lunges that threatened my survival, to pluck each fruit at the peak of its ripening. Decision without thought, I see through the crystal eyes of bug. I see them now, automatic, inborn, smelly, untroubled by decision. And now I understand that their methods were always correct, though each individual instinct could not boast similar perfection; some bugs, after all, are gnashed in the beak of probability or smitten by the shoe of uncalculated omnistasis. My existence, however, is warranted in the binding of perfect response; I am the Bugmeister, terminal surgeon of vermin.

Each second of my actuality synchronously surges into the present, for, I conclude, the Zero Zone bears no room for the roundness and depth of time; the multitudinous layers peel apart and flatten. All at once, I reminisce the full duration of my being, and the emotions this evokes are jagged and unsettling. Now, algorithmically analyzing my existence without the cumbersome obstacle of time, I understand that my life was never my responsibility. It would unfold unto me at one point or another, its decisions written into my blood, and my only course of action was to endure, only holding on to the ever diminishing hope that the scribes of my fate spoke my language. Wanton comes this world, and I to it, unprovoked, uncordial. Though I would have welcomed prenaissance rehearsal, I do not complain. Life will be lived. The mantis will feast.

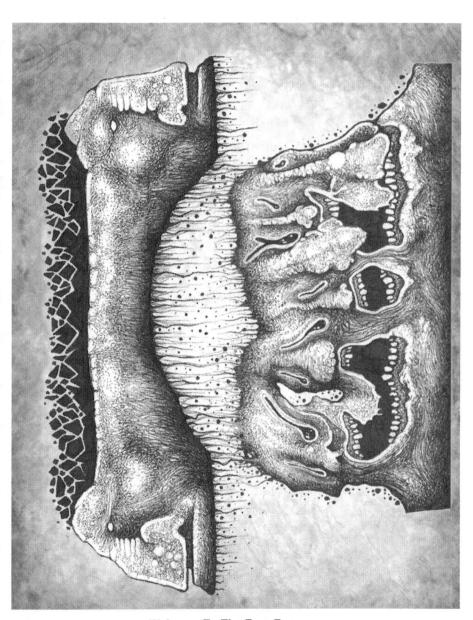

Welcome To The Zero Zone

1: EXCELSIOR

I'm awake in a confusion of echoing waves.

My throbbing mind spins from balance, ripped from sleep,

Drowning, and I'm dragged across shoals of skeletal hands,

Freed from their fleshy sarcophagi,

Smearing lactic acid against my naked teeth.

The nightmare is staring from the hollow in my eyes, perched on the rim of my pupil.

If I looked, I'd see it in the mirror.

It runs through the trees in the night when it rains loud and wild.

Inhaling through an ocular gasp,

It funnels strange company into the subconscious cellar.

The cellar is lost in the abyss that spawns even in the shallow waters of the night

Or peeking through the empty chasms of a broken mirror.

I'm standing now.

I hear all the other corpses rise. The soot stirs.

It is time for labor.

~L.

      The wind's howl roared on through icy teeth, blisteringly frozen, and the post-war's wicked smirk perpetually rattled me. I stumbled outside with the rest of the workforce, still rubbing my tongue with my greasy fingers in an attempt to rinse the stale taste of rust and acid from my mouth. In all my years, I never grew accustomed to the wet, sloshing roar of the miasmic spacecraft that resided in the center of our wretched sector as a disgusting reminder of the war's merciless victor*. The shuttle's originally

11

mighty interior reeked of rancid meat and oxidized metal. Bristly vines intermingled within the loosened buckles and bolts, drenching the ship in thick, gleamous sap. The off-kilter spacecraft had long been hollowed out to accommodate the excess supply of maggots; in fact, the colossal silo, as it came to be known, bred industrial quantities of the larval nightmares. That tilted metal silo of murmuring maggots sat triumphantly erect, planted firmly in a mound of Western dirt. And this beacon of false control, with its rays of confusion, convinced far too many people that they were subject to its demands. It was the holy sword of the Left, embedded in stone. I, however, saw the silo for what it was: an ancient relic, a tribute to the former glory of the Soviets and nothing more. I would not allow some silent monument to extend its influence over me. For I knew that it attempted to establish dominion over a land that could not be tamed. The land remained oblivious to the symbolism that we assigned the spacecraft. Nature was alive—more so than its complacent residents—and it would not accept subservience.

*Once the first nuclear missile detonated in Moscow following the U.S. Military's mix-up in labelling two adjacent buttons, one that initiated total nuclear warfare and another that ordered Chinese takeout, the conflict that had been known as the Cold War took on the more sinister designation of World War Three. A cool, spirited war it had been—one that had recently ceased, ascertaining unquestioned global dominance to the prevailing superpower. The Soviets had triumphed over their eternal western foe, the United North American Provinces, after a hilarious blunder from George Washington himself, having briefly returned from the dead to scare the Red back.

Grunty Kraba, the fourth sector within the southwestern province of what was once the land of the free, hosted the war's final battle on the turn of the century, a mere two years before my unfortunate birth, though attached to that estimate is potential and probable error, since time's pendulum seemed to have long since forgotten to swing in our corner of the globe.

No display of power could have undermined the American spirit more than otherworldly exploration–a commemoration of American failure to conquer the Soviets on the final frontier. The moon's sky was the final resort for the desperate Westerners, since American troops proved grossly inferior on earthly battlegrounds and through all other competitive media, including swagger and popularity. But even the quick space-battle culminated in humiliation. Regretfully, the American engineers used oxygen balloons hanging off the sides of their shuttles to replenish the precious breath of their astronauts once their limited supply within their chambers ran out. After the balloons were untied by a two-man Soviet team, the American engineers admitted the flaw in their design. However, the engineers stood by their blueprints and defended their credentials, crying in accusation: "We anticipated that the Soviets would play by the rules." But they hadn't, and now the sweet land of liberty was just a faraway fable remembered in an old song.

Thus, the globo-Soviet government installed its retired shuttles in every sector of every province, and Grunty Kraba, of course, was no exception; the remains of the Soviets' prized Sputnik tainted the patriotism of our once-democratic seaport town.*

13

Ours was not much of a home; the island of Grunty Kraba was devastated by harsh elements and scattered with little devils sleeping to hide in blankets of unforgiving terrains. The sun sweated lazy rays of infinite heat, drooping down parabolically like a willow tree, for even light energy sagged odiously in the dreadful swelter. Despite the torridity, frigid spells of stinging cold plastered the fields with glacial frost once every moon cycle, destroying the harvest and bludgeoning the wildlife population with a polar fist. The fields remained unsaturated throughout even the heaviest showers. Rain poured from the heavens, but demons scurried puddle to puddle, collecting the water in their bags. Ominous peaks towered above ruthless alpines, giving way to the cruel jungle and the unrelenting marshlands. Even the fairest of the landscapes, the Great Plain, was littered with craters. A peek inside one of these rocky chasms would reveal the acidic sea beneath the Earth. The waves playfully tossed the ever-resounding wails of the damned about in an eternal game of supersonic catch. Roars emulated as serpents splashed in the underworld's coves, and few whose feet slipped through the cracks lived to tell the tale. Few people lived to tell any tales in this world actually, except for me, I suppose.

But while the climate smited Gruntians with an elemental sledge, its meteorologic hegemony was also rivalled by the indisputable political dominance of the Siberian destructors. Grunty Kraba, once a bustling trade city teeming with vivid merchant activity, decayed into a gurgling torrent of pain and poverty after the oligarchic mob infiltrated the system. The series of newly installed leaders rewrote history, falsified documents, and regaled us with tales of their might. But they never considered the tendency of systems to eventually return themselves to their natural state. Nothing can be buried in the past because no time is linear. Soon along the chronological cycle, time would reveal what had been buried long ago. Soon.

2: My Life Is A Pizza Party

Each district became acquainted with its appointed Chancellor of Punishment, and his duties called for the evaluation of every newborn—a Judgement held at every birth. The Chancellor would clothe himself in his court robes, and the newborns would assume their roles as the convicts. Those unfortunate enough to be judged wrathfully would suffer a disgusting, maggot-infested fate. Those unfortunate enough to be "spared", would instead suffer the struggle to survive until experiencing the swipe of the sweet, obsidian scythe of the man in Black.

Krüstof, Chancellor of Grunty Kraba, class-one waddler, had thoroughly satisfied his palette of fancies: artisan glass windows, grand ivory pillars, lush indoor gardens with succulent orchards supporting breeder-sculpted varieties of designer tigers and peaceful songbirds upon which they fed, a seven sided monstro-box conceived by the pinnacle of Persian mathematicians and then constructed by the finest Egyptian engineers, and, according to his top geologists, the oldest rock, which had once been located in the exact center of the Earth *fart noize*. And he even flaunted the world's only pizza parlor, complete with a stainless steel ice machine (Wow!). The parlor had prestige architecture contrived by Archimedes himself, mimicking the likes of the olden day pizza parlors, but, disappointingly, the chefs were ill-equipped, for all recipes of the ancient cuisine had been lost in translation. The last steaming heap of chee-z-za had been whipped up decades ago. Our nostalgia derives in the wild dance of our desire's contemplation. Our lament is the needle that guides the tune from the groove. It's very easy for our hearts to tell the band to play.

Every cantation is a eulogy for the lost generation. *Rest in peace, Pizza Kids; we will miss your birthday parties. We embellish your grave with bouquets of marinara and havartis* [Do you wheeze when you eat cheese? (Delete before publishing)].

It wormwas obvious to Krüstof, based on his collection of antiques and otherwise, that he should be the most popular of the world's Chancellors. After all, who else could boast a severed butt* mounted over his fireplace? However, recent polls suggested otherwise; Chancellor Vultrovort just edged over Krüstof's 400,000,000,000,000 likes to reach a dashing 6.8 octillion, while Chancellor Plupo trailed slightly at a less impressive 5.00×10^1 likes (consult graph). This unfortunate popularity deficit galvanized Krüstof's creation of his very own PR campaign.

> *The Chancellor originally pioneered the delicacy of hindquarter reverence billions of years before a certain aquatic patrician would claim the patent that forever eluded Krüstof.*

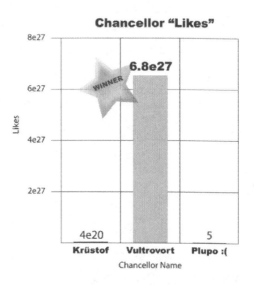

<!-- graph -->

Chancellor "Likes"

8e27

6.8e27

6e27

WINNER

Likes

4e27

2e27

4e20   5

Krüstof   Vultrovort   Plupo :(

Chancellor Name

One device was created to harness the propaganda duties, and it held responsibility for the nautical Chancellor's advertisement. It rode a crude, papier-mâché scooter, but its stubby legs struggled hopelessly to reach the ground, so propulsion typically relied on emphatic rocking to and fro–what must have resulted in agonizing pain for its pitiful seat. A meatmask blotched with white blood stretched over its genetically engineered face; the rider provided to the unwilling and unfortunate onlooker a classic example of Krüstof's maggotial experimentation. Unpolished music blared from the speaker implanted in its unreasonably malodorous maw, but even more unsettling than the queer, Krüstofian rhythms were the muddled ramblings of the Chancellor himself. His voice was dirty and loud.

"You love Krüstof! Everyone sing about your love! Go ahead!" the Mobile Maggoteer–as we came to know him by unfaltering law, though, I must add, labelling so stagnant a creature as "mobile" seems insulting to the word itself–screeched in a voice suspiciously similar to that of our Chancellor. Eurotrash melodies thumped in the fuzzy background of the lowbred speaker, which trumpeted whistles of discordant frequency as often as it did musical notes. Quivering children responded in optimistic fear, hoping in vain that by verbally supporting Krüstof and bouncing in rhythm with the MIDI melody, the Maggoteer would gift them with certificates of extended life; like a morbid readaptation of the alluring tune of the ice-cream truck salesman did the PR specialist captivate infants. Their nasal dismay at the Mobile-Maggoteer's septic breath paralleled their emotional horror as the maggothing gifted only the promise of guaranteed work in the maggot farms or mines–an imbecilic promise to begin with, but one that Krüstof did not even bother to keep. Adults at least mentally acknowledged that the Maggoteer would not ameliorate their circumstances, but even they succumbed to the charisma of implied musical threats, knowing that failure to do so would certainly result in public humiliation and execution.

Krüstof considered the creation of his Mobile-Maggoteer quite ingenious, and he thought it would be quite simple to disguise the being as an ordinary rabbit. His scientists promised Krüstof that they had discovered a compound which would cloak the scooter with invisibility. However, the "cloaking agent" was in reality two sloppy, disappointing coats of dripping silver spray paint. Imagining that his subjects would be too incompetent to spot the blatant obviousness of his invention, Krüstof declared that the pre-recorded applause generated by the speaker actually reflected his citizens enjoying life under his rule. However, some arrogant fatty dared to point out that the "rabbit" was some maggot abomination cooked up in a government lab, adorably fashioned with a bunny nose and tail. Krüstof denied the accusations and set forth the law, criminalizing the action of peeking at the Mobile-Maggoteer. "Curiosity killed the cat," Krüstof reminded us with a wagging finger.
Krüstof exulted in the success of his plan, for all residents of Grunty Kraba claimed that they liked their "cool" Chancellor. But the dimwit later realized that he had already ascertained the loyalty of his subjects long before the ridiculously expensive creation of the Mobile Maggoteer by refusing to dispense voting ballots to his citizens and instead filling out thousands of forms himself. Vultrovort's supporters, not his own, were the ones that would need

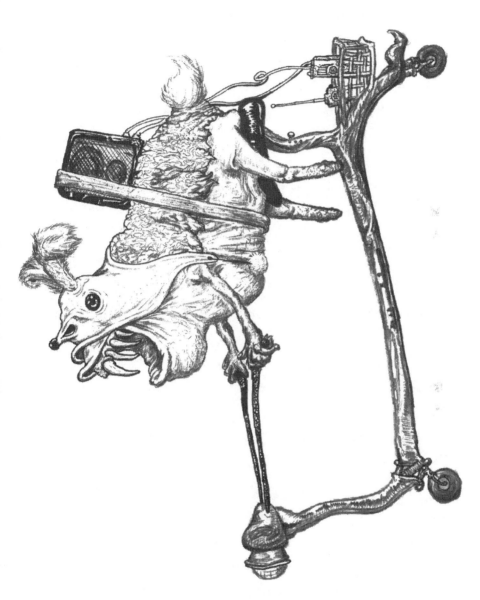

The Mobile Maggoteer

serious convincing. Attempting to locate Vultrovort so as to reroute his Maggoteer to promote his badassery elsewhere, Krüstof whipped out his hand-drawn map depicting the regions of authority of all neighboring Chancellors. Unfortunately, the overconfident crab had irresponsibly waxed over the expanses of Vultrovort and Plupo with cherry crayon, replacing their names with his own in expectation that he would have overtaken their sectors by the time this map would serve him any purpose. In obvious embarrassment, not wanting to reveal his political ineptitude to his savvy council of PR specialists, he arbitrarily assigned the Maggoteer a new itinerary anyways, sending his billion-dollar investment off into the forest to spread the word of the glamor of the Gruntian Chancellor to the uncivilized ears of the bats and the frogs. At least that would come to use, he reasoned, lying flatly to himself as he waited impatiently in his bed, refusing to sleep until someone remembered to tuck him in.

Typically only a small mob of children would peer into Krustof's window as he slept, but this morning, a substantial crowd assembled. Their stomachs slapped them in the face and attempted to swallow their limbs whenever they stopped paying attention; hungry as they were, they ignored their thundering guts and instead fumed at the Chancellor, unable to comprehend his extravagant waste of money on advertisement above food. Knowing that they themselves lacked the combative power necessary to take direct revenge, they looked to Karma to avenge their misery; every morning, the congregation of gaunt children would gather outside Krüstof's palace to watch him sleep, praying that the Puppeteer would cut the Chancellor's string and allow him to slip into death during his slumber.

That particular morning, the expectant younglings observed a queer sagging in Krüstof's eye bags that allowed his pupil to roll ever so slightly into the light. The Chancellor's jaw, too, slacked open, his tongue peeking out of his teeth and drooping against his lip like a bloody stool crowning from a chapped anus. After a few hours of studying this thanatoid positioning, murmurs sputtered through the crowd. The tiny hearts of the starving children mustered an unusually high ten beats-per-minute as a few boys nearly cracked smiles, many beginning to believe that the merciful hand of fate had swept into Grunty Kraba in the night to steal the life from their oppressor. Others were unconvinced, attempting to hush the crowd's premature elation, but secretly harboring a seed of hope themselves, intestines twisting and blood rushing into their throats as they imagined that the Sandman's chariot brandished bayonets on that night as it rode into town to slay the dragon Chancellor.

One audacious boy silenced the crowd with a quivering point.

"The fly..." his voice delicately strummed. The crowd's gaze joined his upon the winged insect that hovered towards Krüstof's body and slowed near his face, finally landing directly upon the Chancellor's exposed pupil. Krüstof did not flinch.

"The Chancellor is dead!" the boy exclaimed, and the children burst into joyous celebration, dancing and weeping and holding each other in disbelief before the corpse for which they had prayed.

Suddenly, like a venus fly trap, Krüstof's fanged eyelids squashed the insect. The rejoicing halted as the bug innards splattered across the window. No one could see through the sap of twitching bug limbs, so a young boy pressed his ear up against the window. Through the hushed breathing of the crowd, the boy heard a thud, and then footsteps, like a train tearing down hot metal tracks. Suddenly, Krüstof's gray, craggy face smashed through the window, gnashing, barking, and biting the boy's ear off. The children's legs carried them far from the window, and they scurried into trash piles like roaches. Krüstof spit the ear out in disgust at the offensive awakening. His feelings were deeply affected. "I'm much too powerful to ever die in my sleep! I'll slaughter all of you!" he bellowed. Perhaps that sounded a bit terrifying, but Krüstof simply became defensive like that when people were mean, O.K.? The Chancellor would not die on that day, but the children all would at his hands.

3: WHEN BISHOPS FALL

Yes, totalitarian power thrived under the bloodthirsty Chancellors. Chancelloric authority surpassed that of punishment only, and their control extended into the fine details of everyday life. Chancellors policed their villages venomously, and unabridged control was soon usurped. However, unity seldom persisted, for a dry old glue stick bound together the global Russian confederacy: the Chancellors had a tendency to war with each other for land and popularity. Indeed, they constantly competed through local tournaments; fashion, singing, dancing, and jumping were common trials for the rulers. Beside the competing chancellors, none were allowed to attend these competitions, and it soon became evident to the public that every Chancellor claimed to have won every challenge. No, the Chancellors soon realized these phony championships would never do to gain popular approval. Even if the masses did believe their Chancellor had prevailed, no Chancellor could in this manner gain appeal with residents of districts outside of their domain, for the leaders of those districts also claimed victory. Instead, new methods of increasing popularity arose, including the use of the newly re-invented television commercial (for, of course, the world had recently entered into the Reverse Industrial Revolution*, in which technology plummeted to history's lowest levels since the 1400s).

*Politicians exhibited extreme confidence
in their own abilities, so they settled all matters
personally rather than through technology; to
prevent heating tensions, all arms races were
halted and dissolved, and, furthermore, reversed,

by a mutual agreement. Some decades before Krüstof's inauguration, three powerful Chancellors known as "Da Big Boyss," a trifecta of political masterminds, monopolized their respective regions and worked together with the less-powerful Chancellors in an effort to ostracize and obsoletize their competitors. In a desperate attempt to tip the scales in their favor, the Boyss funnelled treasury funds, all natural resources, bake sale profits, and even private capital into wildly expensive abstract art projects, proxy jousts, and exotic animal importations. The Boyss, Frimlick Du Whip Wip of the South, Panch "The Dirty Boy" Funt representing the West, and Crispet Rhentle from the North, introduced a spectacular myriad of species ranging from killer bees and Komodo dragons to plush mosses and Indian corn to the territories, considerably boosting their reputations and political power and instilling pride-slashing jealousy in their rivals. Unable to accept the inferiority of his conventional, edible corn, Du Whip Wip dedicated the majority of his speeches and legislation to the widespread public recognition of Funt's "dirty" status. Du Whip Wip's PR specialists even went so far as to create propagandist cartoons featuring Funt kneeling in a waste-bin, wearing a baseball cap backwards. Retaliation included riots in the wasteland border towns, mandatory gender reassignments, and aggressive emails. The most noble method of competing between chancellors, however, was the

Reverse Industrial Revolution. Government-hired thugs burned factories and powerplants down with crudely fashioned molotov cocktails, and inventors were paid handsomely to dismantle technologies screw by screw and forced to loiter and waste time. All inventors were vacuumed by the mouth of unemployment camps soon after their freedom quotas were met. One man, a toothless peasant farmer forced to grow worthless, multicolored Indian corn, became a living legend when he made the ultimate sacrifice in the name of counterscience. Allegedly technologically inept, the self proclaimed "not computer guy" disregarded all foundations of innovation, logic, and human instincts by boiling water within his own two hands over an open flame. Such disinventors received ample bribes from aspiring politicians who sought to eventually reinvent each uncreated technology, thus swinging popular support towards them. Unfortunately, "lazy-affair" is a bible to these comfortable sinners; politicians simply never got around to the whole "reconstruction" spiel.

"I think we all want progressive technology, but not if it's gonna be a whole thing to deal with."
–Rhentle (A Reminder to the Public)*

I recall a very strange day from several elections ago: Plupo snuck his campaign strategists into our sector to broadcast their commercial. The campaign manager, an Easterner, a devil of the Orient, wheeled out the television on a creaky stand and laughed loudly like a silly chinaman full of proverb–like a goofy gook who knew something you didn't. "Come, yes if you want yes, come look you people for yourself to see more! Haha! Look it yourself! He he!"

I gathered with a small crowd around Plupo's men marveling at their television. I was, however, unimpressed by their technology and wished only to see if the other candidates were as horrible as Krüstof. A crackling static zapped the black screen, and animations promptly manifested from the gray glass as the motion picture began. Plupo sat in front of a chess board, and across from him sat a small boy. The skin on the little boy's face seemed to be comprised of the withering tissue of a green and bogwater-filled lung. The child's eye would slouch and ooze to his chin with the slipping folds of his sloppy epidermis. Bizarre batches of fungi bloomed on his wet cheeks; his face was a quilt of decay, and different factions of mushroom fed off the discoloration of the different divisions on the indelicate, verdant display. All the while, as liquefaction of the infected face partook, Plupo sat in silence. He did not go to great length to conceal his gags as the grisly toddler remained unwilling to play his turn. A slop of flesh dripped from the boy's jaw and splattered his pawns; Plupo's face contorted with a disgust that happened to miscarry his intentions to portray a message of kindness. Plupo turned to face the camera. He looked at his viewers and spoke through the puke in his throat: "I love helping kids." He emptied his gullet of the vomit after looking back at the flesh-covered chessboard and then wiped the sweat out of his eyes. The lengthy silence and macabre atrophy of the malnourished

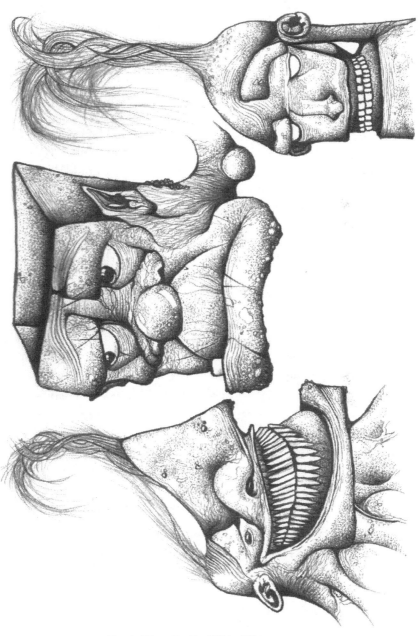

Funt, Rhentle, Du Whip Wip

28

parasite-kid would further shrivel Plupo's popularity ratings—
imminent ruin for the already underdog Chancellor. The crowd
disassembled, leaving the Eastern man alone with his television set.
It wasn't long before the next viewers would begin to gather.

I continued down the road, still hearing the Easterner
pleading for the crowd to return or chanting "Go Plupo! Arregedost!
Vote Plupo the most!" His voice faded, and I marched back into the
suffocating smoke of fossil fuel.

4: Judgement—The Gavel Of The Hive

Yes, there were always incinerators. The ovens could only be used by the Chancellor of Punishment, for as he wandered often through the villages to patrol for infractions, which he seldom overlooked, there was often need of a nearby furnace into which a transgressor could be hurled. Grunty Kraba employed few farmers, for the raging elements mercilessly thwarted any attempt at growing food, squandering all agricultural justice, and so it was not worth dedicating multiple men's lives to the crop; many men were instead assigned to work on the ever-blazing furnaces. Each block boasted its own incinerator, and each was often decked-out and customized before being entered into competitions in which the neighborhood with the most fabulous oven, as chosen by the Chancellor, would receive one bucket of maggots as reward. Of course, no one enjoyed so wriggling a trophy, but they taught themselves to pretend they did, for Chancellor Krüstof often slaughtered anyone who failed to enthuse at the mention of maggots. Multiple men necessarily tended to each bedazzled oven, for the great fires were too ravenous to be tamed by one laborer. They were lined with maggots, but, of course, these were dead and roasted. Once an hour it was necessary for the layer of maggot soot to be replaced with a fresh batch, though I cringe at deeming any variation of these vile beings "fresh." No matter how horrid the maggo-things seemed, none could consider them worthless—maggots combusted at the full efficiency of the coal or charcoal products they replaced. I rolled my tongue out of my maw and scraped off the tar that had amassed from my breathing while strolling around, but the pungent taste of the guck still overwhelmed my taste buds. I was ready to get the crud out of my mouth and stop by home for some grub.

But home was quite a walk from here, I thought, and there rested before me a convenient barrel of scraps anyways. That meal would suffice as much as any other, though the pain of hunger would be replaced by that of indigestion; the food in Grunty Kraba was sloppy and barely solid, boasting a watery consistency, while the only available water was pumped from a thick, murky stream (the Chunky River), and was therefore meaty and mucky, more solid than even the food. Some of the more daring young people were so dehydrated that they would burst into flames after attempting to "soak up some sun." The stream's moisture content may have been high, but it was densely concentrated with sediment, creating a ludicrously amoebic solution of oily mud. Commonly, the abundant supply of maggots fed Grunty Kraba's perpetually ravenous population, and thus nutrition levels reached an all-time local low.

5: THE BEASTS THEY CHAINED

The takeover of this offshore North American wasteland had been rather sudden. Gungo Scuddz, the region's moronic leader at the time of takeover, merely puked like the infant he was as the Chancellor of the time, Tarbeerioid the Pig, single handedly dragged an inflatable concentration camp over the island. Instead of poking the camp with a needle, residents of Grunty Kraba attempted to play Jump-O! on what they presumed to be an inappropriately gloomily tinted bouncey-house; all who participated faced instant death, for Tarbeerioid, a total grump-boy, hated happiness, especially aerial-bound entertainment. The needle would have proven fatal to the entire operation, which I must say was horrendously under planned, though still effective enough to enslave the entire island. Only two areas of the makeshift death place were not off-limits: The Yard and The Darkroom.

Father A01 was a Yard-dweller when I was born, but his place neared the bottom of the hierarchical dominance tree. He belonged to a class of barely acceptable Yardlings—men dangerous enough to repel predators but lacking sufficient strength to defeat another Yardling in combat. Above them were multiple stout, chunkoid men aggressive enough to keep the higher-ranked outlaws on their toes, and should any of the unquestionable apexes suffer an injury or incapacitation, these second-tier Yard-dwellers would voraciously pounce to fill the power vacuum. Providing stark contrast to The Yard's zenith of impeccably formed, bloodthirsty criminals existed the sucklings that inhabited The Darkroom; these were a blobbish, unfortunate, wheezing race of malformed wormishes accurately classified as defensive-types for their pacifist

32

nature, though not even the greatest Yard-dweller would dare confront one of these in combat. Physical battling would entail entering The Darkroom, and to do so, having been so perpetually accustomed to the sensory stimuli of The Yard, would bring about certain insanity to even the healthiest mind. Indeed, there roamed no light in The Darkroom—none would dare enter—though somehow still the most terrifying and psychologically destructive sights were seen. There existed no odors, though any who accessed the room would instantly have lost their sense of smell due to the sheer rancidity of the air alone, and, if they had ever been able to find the exit, they would quickly have noticed the uselessness of their tarnished noses. There sounded no sounds, but the most horrifying of screams—the kind that plagued the nightmares of even the manliest being, wrenching profuse tears out of infant and beast alike—rattled against the bleeding eardrums of all trespassers. Suffocating ink enveloped all; a dry breath was an unknown luxury. Hallucinations galore tormented the powerful mind to gradual insanity and dangled suicidal temptations that the feeble mind could not resist. Poisonous air, bleeding water, breathing darkness, psychopathic humidity. Almost as deadly as the elements, the occupants wetly chomped on intruders within their personal and metaphorical bubbles with tiny, sharp teeth, connected flimsily to weak, snow-white skin. Even so, many preferred the hazards of The Darkroom to the permanent warfare of The Yard, where severed limbs and popped skulls littered the crimson landscape as maniacal warlords chuckled heartily while they feasted on the flesh of their inferior victims.

6: ONE FOR THE FODDER

Early in my childhood, it became evident to me that the family unit, established prior to the Third World War, decomposed upon Soviet seizure of global power. Mothers, for example, faced imminent extinction; each sector brandished one female breeder from whom all infants spawned. This innovation came about as a solution to end mass famine, for with only one female necessary per sector, all feminine infants recycled into the food supply. Additionally, since the breeder could only produce one child per nine months, except for in the rare instances of twins or triplets, population never experienced an increase that would have proved impossible to sustain with the limited food supply, for the war had proven fatal to nearly all plant and animal life. Fathers came and went. Seldom did a child boast his biological father, for Chancellors killed adults often, even if they executed perfect performance (recorded in their conduct logs). Instead, fathers would often be assigned to many unrelated children (though, of course, all children were technically half-siblings, since they all bore the same mother), and upon the arrival of a new father, each child received a debriefing packet with all necessary information regarding their new paternal figure: favorite food—which was invariably maggots, by law—maximum jump-height, and identification code—three letters/digits by which the child could distinguish his father from the rest of the gray, Gruntian biomass. A mere three weeks into my life, I first witnessed the Chancellor of Punishment penalize the ignorance of my biological father (identification code A01).

How woeful a day it was when mortality's morbid intervention aligned the stars to strike upon the diurnal course, on the third thrice morn of an ominous winter. The news reached the public ear through the Non-livers' section of the weekly paper on the twenty-first day of my life. My own cousin had been fed to the writhing wriggle worms of the silo–the maggots. Winter fell late on the year my father departed from the mortal realms; it was still fall, and the autumn leaves glided upon the air like amber kites. The crisp grass crunched mildly as I strode on all fours across the fields to the silo. I was but an infantile apprentice, already learning the craft of our village from my original father, who stupidly thought he could teach adult customs to a creature struggling even to crawl. My biological father was commanded by the crusty old crab-man, Krüstof, to unscrew the bolts on the top of the silo containing the maggot spawn.

Krüstof, the village elder and the Chancellor of Punishment, conducted such executive decisions as deeming newborns fit* or unfit to serve.

> *RECALL: If deemed fit, they would join the Youth Education Program, assuming the simple training necessary to claim the mundane lifestyle of a maggot breeder–an existence of sorrow and darkness. If the newly birthed vaginal spud-lump was deemed unfit, it became fodder for the maggots.*

The silo's lid, per Krüstof's orders, would be removed and the interior revealed to the heavens; gods would bury their faces in the clouds and weep as they saw evil soaking in their canvas and bleeding into their reproductive art. As the obedient worker removed the lid, Krüstof would release the month's load of worthless baby children into the gaping maw of the silo, and infants would sink through the thick layers of maggot as the worms picked at their flesh

35

until they were recycled through the glorious process of decomposition—not to be confused with the process of the Nitrogen Cycle, which many scientists have discovered to be another fallacy from the false prophet Daniel Rutherford. The maggots could be heard squirming, making moist sounds as they rubbed each other. My father patrolled the brim of the silo on lid duty—his natural position for which he sported uncanny talent. He crouched ferally for maximum lifting power as he hunched down to grasp the unbolted lid. Krüstof stood watching with the same beady eyes of a crow as he perched on the silo's ledge behind my father.

"Lift", Krüstof gruffly bellowed out with a mild wheeze and a wet cough. Father A01 jerked his spine and flipped the lid backwards, revealing the silo's feared interior. Krüstof's smile became crooked, and his toothy grin extended to either ear. He knelt and reached into the burlap sack which encased the squealing mass of human infants. He tossed them in, one by one, until only one was left: cousin Roveleek. Krüstof handed the baby to my father and commanded him to toss it into the maggots below. My father somewhat nobly refused to dispose of his brother's child, though his unfeeling coldness in aiding infanticide for so many years *almost* made me question his character. He sobbed as he cradled the also weeping child; tears blurred his vision, and he blinked in attempt to drain his flooded see-lookers. He sternly rotated on one foot to turn and deny Krüstof's request, but as he did so, Krüstof reared back with his cane and delivered unto him an assertive, precise nut-tap. In an agonized involuntary reflex, my father launched the tender babe. Roveleek whirled towards me and ended with a bonk. My father swiftly managed to grasp the rim of the silo, toes sizzling in the frictional heat from the beasts below. Krüstof triumphantly stepped up to my dangling father, and he gently cooed: "Accuracy is key!" He slammed the silo's lid on my father's fingers, and they sliced cleanly off and assembled themselves in a neat row. The Chancellor scooped up the digits and dispersed them unto the crowd below, proudly declaring his own benevolence. "Fingers for all! Fingers for all!" The populous roared with delight. So died a worthless, lame man with whom I am 34% hesitant to announce my blood relation.

7: Lost Are The Pure

Many more fathers met their demise in the coming years. They did not matter to me; they were weak, unassertive, squishy men, ignorant and accepting, groveling and appreciative. They lacked hatred, anger, lust... But while I wept not for the loss of my fathers, that of my only friend wrenched more moisture from my eyes than I had suspected sloshed within my entire body. The vivid memory of his youthful screams as I left him that day haunted me until and beyond his eventual death, and I forever remembered every detail in crystalline agony.

The two of us ventured through the thick foliage. Furtive brambles, veiled by the underbrush, clawed at us, flecking our boyish ankles with embryonic scrapes. The thorny branches only teased us, playfully whipping at our skin without drawing blood, tickling at our flesh while shying away from playing too roughly. The canopy of pines sheathed us from the sun and suspended us in dim light. Randomly, sun rays breached the bushy webs of intertwined pine needles which interlocked in a mesmerizing fashion. These thorny organs of the wilting trees quilted into a shadowy, verdant tapestry, and the golden light rays which pierced the branchy canopy sparsely dotted the forest's floor like the freckled cheek of a pasty-faced plumpkin. Amadeus took point, leading us into the soul of forest reaches.

Sweet Amadeus was my childhood friend hailing from the neighbor farm. We met the day I discovered him entangled within the iron clasps of the barbed wire that distinctly established the boundaries between the lands to which our families individually tended for the unquestionable good of the sector. He painted to onlookers the ideal image of adolescent innocence and curiosity. His guru had forewarned him to reside only in the perimeters of their farm, he once explained to me, though his intentions for exploration were pure and fundamentally altruistic. Ever since that day we would travel together, journeying through the outskirts of our residence and sneaking off naively, avoiding the watchful eyes of our fathers.

Now, he slinked awkwardly ahead, his bony arms swaying fluidly and aerodynamically, conforming to the domain of the wind. His features were hollow and sunken with extreme exaggeration; his breast beetled like two skeletal hands adjoining fingers in an eternal clasp; his skin had a ghoulish green glow and tenaciously adhered to the contours of his bone, for there was no flesh to grip. His face was long; his chin protruded boldly to the equator of his nipples. His overweening nose hung flatly against his face, and his ovular cheeks were defined and full, overwhelming his uniformly polygonal facial features. His firm jowls compressed his eye-sockets betwixt the corners of his nasal bridge and his overbearing brow, restricting his vision and forcing his eyes to cross like an autistic yokel in a permanent squint.

As we hiked further through the trees, my head dangled and studied the pine needle surface of the ground, visually combing for interesting artifacts in the areas on which the beacons of sunspots shone.

Suddenly, I noticed that the crunching of pine needles beneath the feet of Amadeus halted. Just before I could lift my head, I collided with his brittle spine and stumbled backwards with a goofish guffaw. I approached him and scanned the dense

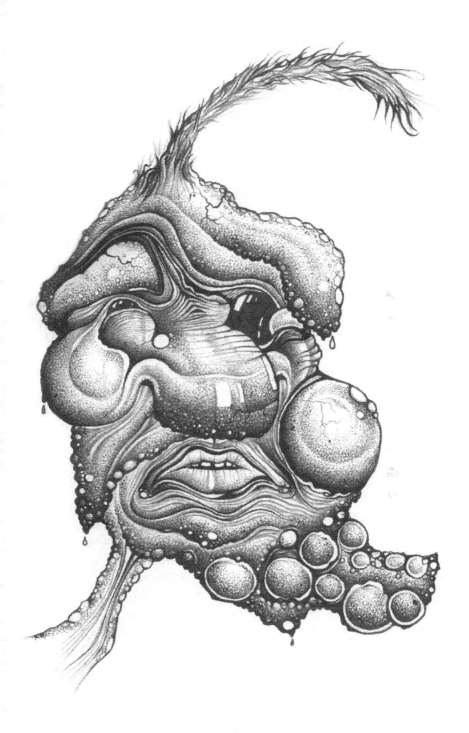

Amadeus

shrubbery, finally discovering the petite clearing upon which his eyes fixated. A single heavenly ray illuminated the clearing and its glorious surroundings. We drew near, orbiting it cautiously and then falling into its gravitational intrigue. The unconditional rain of sunlight blended the objects of the clearing into a warm glow of blurred cream that richly contrasted the motley background, and the sun tenderly caressed our napes as we bent forwards and examined the litter of industrial waste from times long passed. We scavenged through the rubbish, periodically breaking to play with our discoveries. Our wild imaginations molded simple garbages into swords and shields; we fashioned metal rods and wires into grand weapons worthy to be wielded by the wiliest of warriors. We playfully jousted, teasing as we continued our search to better our inventory and advance our armory. We were the proudest champions.

Then Amadeus fell silent, failing to return or even to acknowledge my comical jests, no matter how professionally hilarious and comedy-club-worthy they were. He reached for something amongst the saplings and turned to present it to me, proudly displaying a large, crumpled bag.

This was unlike any other bag we had ever seen. It was not a bag of burlap or wool, but instead a mechanically fabricated bag of plastic, and it crinkled as Amadeus spun with it. This was a relic from days of old, when there were factories and commercial farms before the wars. Amadeus twirled gayly and exclaimed that it would be his futuristic cosmonaut suit. He crawled into the bag and became absorbed by it. He jiggled around wildly to entertain me, jerking left and right and rolling about. Soon his repetitive wobbling

41

maneuvers grew bland, however, and I flatly demanded he remove himself, denying him the politeness of merely asking.

"I'm trying!" he stuttered, and his rising concern became obvious. He grumbled, distraught with fear, groping the bag wildly, but he could not find the hole through which he entered. He was like a frenzied child dressing himself for the first time, lost in his shirt and cramming his head through the sleeve, muttering incoherences of discontent and anxiety. Even his groans themselves wheezed asthmatically as his panic evolved into the exasperation of constriction and inescapability, and his strident oinks fooled nearby pigs into thinking he was one of their mates. I had to save Amadeus. With one hand, I juggled the salvageable keepsakes of the trash pile–small trinkets and plastic silverware; with my other, I heaved Amadeus, still trapped in his confusing entanglement.

I fled to the village, hauling Amadeus along the searing earth, to seek help. Amadeus left blotches of melted skin along the creases of the bag as he dragged against the boiling dirt, but he maintained a forced smile throughout. I could not turn to Father B09's assistance, for if he discovered that Amadeus and I had been off dilly-dallying and not farming, he would surely feed me to the maw of our province's maggot silo.

I finally reached the stoop of the doctor's store front, and, leaving Amadeus behind me at the patio steps, I rapped at the door. I'd heard much of the fame of this skilled practitioner, his prestige elevating him to the honorable duty of operating on even the Chancellor of Punishment himself. He used primitive techniques combined with healing herbs, potions, and crude surgical equipment to treat his patients, but even these meager tools sufficed, for his dexterity was plentiful and his adaptive ability abundant. With a simple glance, he versed himself precisely with the anatomy of any patient. But a passing man called out to me from the streets:

"If you are looking for Doctor Minchus-Watlee, your luck has run dry, boy," he spat. Astonished, I peered into the window to seek confirmation of this seemingly ludicrous statement. The Doc was an amicable man, so much so that we'd developed for him the endearing nickname of "Pons" (very cute name); he always tended willfully to his subjects, and the surgical procedure Amadeus required was one of mediocre difficulty, though no other villager could have hoped to accomplish it. Surely the Doc could spare a moment's inconvenience to grant a boy his companion! Peering in, intrigued and concerned, I noticed that the interior appeared gravely still and eerily dark. No lit candles during business hours–strange. Many would have assumed he was closed or on leave, though I unfortunately knew something unspeakable had occurred, for it was illegal to leave one's work during any hour but that of midnight. No individual, I remembered, no matter how cool or popular, could hope to ignore any article of legislation.

I saw the doctor. He reclined in his seat, soaking in the dripping cushion of his own sour blood. His life pooled in his eyes, unwilling to be sacrificed during the leap from the rotting sockets into the afterlife. He stared at me as I observed his corpse from the window, and he bounced his pupil from side to side, trying to signal to me that he was in fact and unfortunately dead. Whatever was left of his old soul was crucified on his cornea. I choked at the sight of his mangled neck, hunching dramatically as I turned and gagged. Pons Minchus-Watlee ascended gleefully, evoking my utmost envy. But

Dr. Pons Michus-Watlee

my jealousy evolved through a complex emotional natural selection into despair. No man alive could have then surgically removed Amadeus. I feared I could not tear the plastic material, and I searched tearfully for an entrance in the grocery bag but found none; it had simply disappeared, and I was left to wonder how Amadeus entered in the first place.

I lingered in the village for a number of days, seeking medical attention for my friend. Father B09 would not realize my absence amongst his fourteen sons, and even if he did, it was not unusual for a child to be kidnapped by trolls for several days and then to be turned loose again. Amadeus sat in his bag yelping and squealing as he suffocated, but the uncaring pedestrians paid us no mind while I dried my tears on the dirt they kicked into my face. I watched the village people as I slouched next to my friend—a luxury that none of the townsfolk had, for federal decree abolished the concept of amity, and the villagers learned that this embargo on friendship existed for wise reasons. Only efficiency and self improvement mattered, I learned from them. Companions would serve no good except as an anchor; squandering valuable time on the nonsense of a friend would be ineffective foolery. I realized my time was wasting and abandonment was inevitable, so I lugged Amadeus back into the forest, where I knew he would prefer to spend an immobile eternity; it was his most favorite adventure, after all, and at least now he could live it forever. There I departed from Amadeus, severing our ties until some undisclosed date.

Some say Amadeus did find the mouth of the bag that imprisoned him, but his escape was deterred when told by a passer-by that he was to reside in the bag for at least a few years. These people claim that he remained in the bag because he never failed to obey orders, for, Amadeus had always reasoned, doing what one is told is doing one's moral duty. This story I can neither confirm nor deny, but, I can say, it is not one I would rule out of reality, for Amadeus did abide by this exact philosophy of morality.

How I always regretted my decision to leave my sweet 'Deus that day. Only weeks after that did Krüstof build towering barriers separating the fields and the forest, making my journey back to the place of my friend's then-permanent residence impossible. I soon yearned tremendously for my beautiful Amadeus, unable to return to him, and unable to rescue him from his endless entrapment.

8: To Sully One's Hands

It was no mere coincidence that Krüstof enacted these security reformations before I could return to Amadeus, for only months before had I struck a wound deep into his barnacle-encrusted heart.

My Pap Pap—as I endearingly labelled Father B13, seeing him as a drastic improvement above my previous dozen fathes—sat silently, legs crossed in his brown corduroy chaps. Brother sniffled pitifully in the trash can. We had just lost another child to the surprise traffic that buffeted our clan's numbers; thus, the village mother musted birth like a wishfully promiscuous R-strategist. My fetusest siblings brawled silently amongst the carpet moss, but Pap Pap ceased their cacophonous horseplay with a lengthy and glaring hiss, and his tongue slithered as wildly as did the serpentine hate in his eyes. He was so fucking sick of those fags.

I hoisted up my sack, slung it over my shoulder, and fastened my spatula holster securely to my burlap pantaloons, which flowed like great Viking masts billowing towards their petrified victims. I lunged at a rhatt—a genetically engineered novelty animal formulated by Krüstof's regime. Created in a lab with harsh chemicals and cold microtweezers, its life was a scurrying hellscape of hereditarily misplaced agony. I slashed its jugular with my farming spatula.

"I deliver you from suffering, poor rodent fiend," I breathed mercifully. They—the rhatts—infested our humble bungalow until one could not tip-toe across the floorboards without crushing thousands of their young. Amadeus had once recounted to me his father's description of their descendents: the once-extant rats of the days of

47

A Rhatt

48

old had been so elegant and warm, so colorful and wet. They had not seen factories, I assumed. They were not laborious–not efficient. I wanted to escape from the scolding, from the annoyances of the little ones, but the biting chill of the dry winter forbade my departure almost as much as did the speeding automobiles that barreled directly through our farm. Working the arid land amidst the breakneck speed at which government vehicles travelled posed extreme danger to the Chłopak child laborers; I had lost over ten siblings to the reckless drivers. With no roads at all, government officials exclusively allowed themselves to own and operate cars in whatever manner they wished, with no speed limits, stopping, or directional guidelines. Some even afforded portable record players in their cars. Officials could save massive amounts of gas by driving a beeline from point A to point B directly through any foliage, homes, or people in their paths. Steering wheels were haphazardly turned in the destination's direction, and gas pedals were irreversibly pinned to the car floor until the ride's end, like that of a nakajima fighter. For a moment, as I removed an infant from gnawing at my shin, tossing it into the garbage pile across the room, I considered avoiding the perils of the outdoor highways and remaining in the slightly safer home, where only the most daring racers would stick their bumpers. But when I noticed that Pap Pap's blood had spilled into his eyes and flushed his cheeks, signalling a turn of mood into his occasional cannibalism, I decided to take my chances out on the farm. I observed Pap Pap plucking two particularly rambunctious babies from the folds of his back fat and dropping them into his stomach without a qualm of guilt, Moloch's irascible laughter booming through the floorboards. With this sight, I affirmed my suspicions, now determined to take my leave.

I crept towards the doorway surreptitiously, hoping to avoid Pap Pap's gaze. I looked over my shoulder and scanned the room for his potato-bod as a faceful of fingers shattered my cheek. Pap Pap barked, blood dripping from his hanging lip.

"I am… to work," I stammered, anxious. He glared into my very soul and melted my confidence with a terrifying leer. He suddenly lightened and chuckled heartily, delivering a friendly, good-natured punch upon my nose.

"There is no meat," I reminded him. "I cannot bring you any meat. They are out of meat."

He spat in my face and burst into uncontrollable laughter, watching in admiration as I stumbled through the doorway in pain and confusion. He was not a good man, but he was one of the lesser-rotted fruits of our rancid society, and I did almost care for him. I smiled back at him and rubbed my nose as I proceeded.

I wallowed about our meager terraces into the rock fields. "Crucial" accurately describes the task with the fortune of bearing my assignment: I was to flip the rocks when they were ready. I hated terracing the flat land; creating sharp elevational schisms necessary for the terraces with a thirty-six year old spatula proved hard on the callouses. Rock farming failed to entail a prestigious lifestyle, "but it was the lifestyle for me," Father B13 had sternly reminded me on my twelfth birthday—the first and last time he ever talked to me. Corn or cabbage could not grow on account of the farms' freeway double function, for anything we grew would be instantly ravaged by the screaming rubber, the wails of which rivalled those of Mother Earth under humanity's demonic chewing. But rocks… yes, these would grow happily in even this mechanically smited environment.

I noticed that a rock was overdone and picked it up, relocating it into my sack. The typically magnanimous Father A21 would not be happy with my negligence, but his fat ears would never collect my confession on the matter; I assigned it to my mental cabinet marked "Secrets and Unutterances." Finished stones weighed mightily down my aching back, but miles upon miles of fields remained that had yet to be flipped and sacked.

I slung the sack over my shoulder just as a buzzing 1919 Ford Model T whizzed behind me. I made a fraction of a moment's eye contact with the driver just before the misfortunately slung sack annihilated his doughy forehead. The side mirrors barely skimmed my billowing pantaloons, but the windshield failed to evade my rock sack with equivalent grace; the heavy stones easily shattered the glass along with his equally brittle skull. Chunks of solemn stone and shards of neatly apportioned glass buffeted the bewildered driver. The vehicular ruin effortlessly swiped the one-hundred-something pound sack—which epicly collided with and plunged through the unlucky driver's face, blinding and bludgeoning him into a feeble squirt—from my surprisingly unscathed shoulder. The loose burlap, torn open upon impact, clung to his face and flapped over his eyes as he veered to the left, and the stones flattened his cranium like a dumbbell dropped on a crusty raisin soufflé. Bits of his brain splattered my hard, pre-adolescent body. My lips pursed slightly and my eyebrows rose, yet I was unamused as I watched the wrecked vehicle roll off through my farm. I did not move or look away until a mighty oak of six-hundred years finally halted the roadster. The car exploded, and flame showered the magnificent tree. I sidestepped a hunk of blazing debris and flipped a rock with my spatula.

The symphonic crash and following composure of pyrotechnics prompted me to write a poem titled "The Botanical Miracle." For my eyes only.

I twirled my spatula as I neared the vehicle, and it seemed as though Pap Pap's interest had similarly panged. He stood by me as we watched the body inside roast. When the flames finally deflated into embers, after a thorough flambéing, Pap Pap dragged the daredevil out of his infernal chassis by the scorched genital. The charred visage of one of Krüstof's six deformed sons failed to return a gaze into Pap Pap's equally dead eyes.

"Do not worry," a passing stork reassured me. "He is for the maggots now. Krüstof will not care." We left his flame-ridden carcass to rot in the sizzling heap of molten steel and leather, and we children enjoyed his sacrificial warmth. The sun set soon that day.

When I returned to my bungalow, I scanned the dark room to see the shadowy piles of my siblings sleeping. Tranquility at last. I relaxed and nearly dozed off.

Suddenly, I drew a breath fast with fear; some object lashed against the bedroom door, and the thud seemed forceful enough to tear the door from its hinges, but my brothers slept undisturbed. Perhaps my best defense was to play opossum? Yes. So I lay down stiff in my bed and forced my eyes closed. I heard the door creak open and mightily clenched my eyes shut, but I did not hear the footsteps follow into the room as I had anticipated. I manually peeled one eye open and allowed my gaze to tiptoe to the bedroom door. It had swung completely open, and there rested a large rhatt nailed above the door knob. I inspected the creature through a hole in my tattered linens. Its hair was shedding quickly, gathering in smelly, wet clumps on the floor. I watched the individual tufts float down through the sweet air tainted with rancid blood and spoiled meat. Then through the shower of hair, Krüstof lept through the doorway with a pistol aimed into my bed.

"Where is my boy?" he croaked with anger resonating through his froggy voice. I awoke, but not in a sweat. Death had stalked my thoughts, ignoring the private access sign on the side of the road. The Reaper travelled into some crevice of my mind and buried himself there, then coming to linger in my dreams. There would come a day, I decided, when I would return the favor and haunt death with my presence. From that day forward, I became mortal.

Despite my fantasies, Pap Pap had been correct; Krüstof paid no mind to his son's death. In fact, it is unlikely that he ever knew his son's name, and likely that he hated him, for his physical deformities disgraced his family name. But the production of cars was slow in Grunty Kraba, and this particular model had cost so ample a portion of the sector's revenue that Krüstof had been forced to melt the steel supports of his mansion to build the frame, thus weakening the house substantially and jeopardizing its security; any heavy load exceeding the weight of a neighborhood talking bird would have thereafter been enough to topple its foundation.

53

Krüstof knew some foolish child was accountable for this. And so, although failing to derive telepathically that I, Larwa, specifically bore responsibility for this economically devastating endeavor, he wrathfully erected barriers in spiteful vengeance for the loss of his expenditures, knowing most boys spent their leisure time in the forest. How I yearned for the emergence of some soul righteous enough to put Krüstof in his rightful place—beneath the dirt upon which he never deserved to tread.

9: COCOA SOIRÉE

But perhaps, I reasoned, that soul would never return. Walk upon this dirt it once did, I had been told, and I feared that spirits like his graced the planet with their physical presence once in a lifetime. Indeed, there once existed a creature with daring enough a personality to challenge the Chancellor. The government had yet withstood all attempts at rebellion with comical ease and delight at their ability to obliterate any glimmer of hope the rebels may have momentarily retained; all but one, that is: that of Ślimak Chłopak, my brother.

Ślimak and I never exchanged conversation, for I had yet to gather enough courage to speak to the beautiful man when he left this world for the sweet beyond. Whether he was my biological brother or merely another random, fatherless child appointed to my household, I never discovered, but in our clan his exploits were the stuff of legend. Uncle Rocco often entertained me, upon my specific request, with the myth surrounding his life, and though I knew each word by heart, his story never ceased to fascinate me.

As I did every day, I stood at the forest wall, contemplating, remembering. I thought of Amadeus, of the Chancellor. The wind nipped at my rear end, but I was uninterested in play, and I swatted it away with a grunt. I thought of my brother, and I turned around to face Rocco.

"Uncle Rocco, do tell it! Do tell for me the tale of Brother!" I pleaded, stomping in frustration, anticipating rejection. Rocco stared back at me with a stoic, unmoving expression.

"Oh, don't be a stone man! Please!" Silence met my cries. But after a time, Rocco nodded subtly, consenting to my pleas.

Ślimak's tale, however, could only be communicated through nearly indecipherable movements for fear of governmental repudiation. Indeed, the telling of Ślimak's heroism had long since been illegalized, for his actions reminded the village people of their inspirational Ghost Boy—a legendary figure whose myth Krüstof went to great lengths to suppress. So Uncle danced away, my interpretations of which became the fable:

On a warm, humid day of mid-winter, when the maggots were ripe and bodacious, and when the silo cringed in cramping contortions as it yearned wretchedly for a sloppily constituted victim to fall prey to infraction, Ślimak slipped his way betwixt the velvet ropes guarding the entrance of Krüstof's embassy. An underly-cynical security system, perhaps, but then again, none had ever dared cross Krüstof directly. It was the day of the egging, when all flies would birth their grimy puss babies, thus meriting grand governmental celebration. The feast consisted of only one ingredient: semi sweet chocolate—an incredibly expensive import on which the government had splurged billions of dollars for one night of despicable gorging. The heat was unbearable, despite the time of year, and neither the chocolate nor the attending nobles' internal fat reserves could maintain a solid consistency. The latter failed to remain unhidden, for the odometer reading reached record levels of basicity (likely due to the drastic increase in maggot importation, evident in the consequential increase of ammonia levels in the residents' skin and sweat). The once richly solidified slabs of cleanly cleaved chocolate now poured messily over Krüstof's carpet, but he did not mind, for this was a joyous day filled with the merriest of treats. Little did he know of Ślimak's surreptitious entrance to his abode, dragging a rope ominously tied to the base of the already rusted and dangerously creaking maggot silo, weakened from years of abrasion under the relentless elements of sweltering Grunty Kraba.

Krüstof's embassy radiated scalding heat, broiling and sweating mercilessly under the sun's squalid brilliance. His guests entertained themselves with an infantile gusto, playing with and tossing handfuls of melted chocolate in a voluptuous trance. Their chapped lips puckered meatily as their moist faces contorted in anguish from the sticky air, yet they found a certain comfort in swaddling the rich, thick chocolate. They piled chunks hastily, attempting to overcome its liquidity and construct galleries of amateur cocoa sculptures. They cooed gently and tip toed with delicate enthrallment as their manual delight surrounding the chocolate became paralleled by an equally amusing pedecacao fetish. Relishing the moisture between their toes, they lightly danced upon pools of chocolate, splashing their emaciated bones crunchily and grinding away their last reserves of joint cartilage, for their lanky limbs included nothing but haggard bones, deteriorated after years of calcium deficiency. They did not taste the treat, however. For, after hours in the hot room with sweaty government officials who were drenching themselves odorously in the blackening muck, beads of ammonia-contaminated perspiration dripped into the rank, brownish-green chocolate solution, suggesting that the volcanic conditions, which provided ample breeding grounds for various mosses and fungi, rendered consumption of the delicacy fatal.

57

The Egging

58

Face caked-over in dried cocoa grease, Krüstof's comatosed maw involuntarily dripped saliva. His drooping eyelids dapped rapidly as he drifted into slumber, a lone sailboat breaching the benign horizon. In this delusional reverie, he sat alone in his great dining hall, feasting still, but the chocolate was gone. It was all meat, raw and moist, pure and glorious. It was all his, audibly challenging him to devour it all in one sitting. Being a supreme athlete (though now desperately overweight) trained to annihilate such an undertaking as this, Krüstof dove, sprawling on the juicy sustenance like a ravenous alligator death-rolling a feeble fawn on the low banks. He gurgled on the chewed meat, hacking and grunting through the digestive strife. The meat was stacked high for tables upon tables, brimming over onto the floor. Unfortunately, however, his gluttonous glee transmogrified into flabbergasted dolor, for the meat was all gristle. Convulsing in an embonpoint sweat wad was, from his third-person viewpoint, his sleeping conscious, which could not determine if the sinewy knots of fat or the vice-like pincer grip autodispatched upon his windpipe clogged his throat. As he watched himself die, slowly and alone, surrounded by his avaricious superabundance, he realized that this bizarre fantasy paralleled his reality all too scrupulously. He awoke with a start, coughing and sputtering chocolate all over his lifeless guests. Semi-liquid chocolate dripped from the ceilings, falling into snoring kissers that dehisced around his embassy of filth. There was no meat and no gristle, but chocolatey goo presided honorably over the assembly in tons, so much so, in fact, that Krüstof's home began to moan as the foundations wobbled* under the immense weight.

RECALL: the house's foundation had already been wounded by the wasteful use of its metal to create the automobile I had destroyed.

But over the hundreds of soft screams from the chocolate-aficionados, none detected their imminent destruction; none could have foreseen the ease with which Ślimak could now destroy the establishment.

The silo gave way easily enough, its rusty constitution giving out and collapsing with one violent tug of the rope that Ślimak wielded. The tower toppled over onto the chocolate-infested embassy, which proved even simpler prey and even less fortified; the maggots–not so much. They came in millions, clumping into starchy boulders, densely penetrating the weak establishment with vascular finesse. A sea of ammoniac secretions trampled the party guests, their hollow, malnourished bones providing no resistance to the wave of larvae. Most officials exploded instantly, releasing their life-blood and brain matter into the already atrocious mix of chocolate, sweat, mold, and maggots. Others were crushed to death loudly by the heavy mass of maggots, fracturing and compacting into splintered bone lumps as shards of shattered skull gave way to leaking marrow. Most maggots exploded into hundreds of damp pieces, chunkily leaking thick maggo-pus, and their pulverized remains formulated grubish pulp, further fattening the solution. The larval survivors were no less grotesque, devouring any human resistance along with the already dismantled carcasses of former officials. Bit by bit the maggots overtook the foundation, bending steel and crumbling concrete. Only Krüstof, slathered in maggot paste, managed to escape their wrath. His chiseled fist tore through maggot bodies briskly, plowing incisively into the maggot brigade as if his knuckles were freshly oiled cavalry. Thus he survived, punching the disgusting critters to death and clawing his way up the treacherous climb to his dilapidated roof. Krüstof's triumphant grin faded after only a brief spell, for Ślimak's watchful eye never failed to capture through the periphery, and Krüstof's not-so-stealthy escape did not go unnoticed. Ślimak ran.

Krüstof's corpulent excellency could not compete with Ślimak's pubescent form, flowering with graceful strokes of athleticism. Ślimak ran vigorously, pumping rippling muscle into pure energy, striding forth to avoid his incarceration, and his mouth salivated at the thought of imminent government shutdown. Krüstof gathered a handful of stones and hurled them in Ślimak's direction. No stone made it ten feet from Krüstof's palm. Krüstof knew he was outmatched in a fair fight, and his only hope would be treachery or deceit.

The Chancellor placed his claw against his temple and thought of Kambu, the supreme shaman. Although the shaman had not been present before Krüstof summoned him, once the Chancellor had officialized his mental request, Kambu not only manifested at that moment but also did so at all times before then; he had now been there forever, since before the chocolate party, before Krüstof had been born, before Kambu himself even existed.

"Kombo!" the Chancellor exclaimed.

"You have spoken first, crab-child!" reverberated Kambu's voice from all angles of the field. His lips maintained their eternal, virgin rest.

"Can you help me kill him? Please? I was really nice today," Krüstof pleaded, pointing at Ślimak accusingly. Then, attempting to appeal to the shaman after noticing his apparent indifference, he added: "To an old guy."

"The spirits give nothing freely. You bargain with a priceless refuge of your mind, nematode." foreboded Kambu. The cryptic warning caused Krüstof's eyeballs to swell.

The shaman tossed his gaze against the skies, whereupon his celestial doppelgänger loomed in the parallel of the shadow dimension. Kambu's ray of vision energy ricocheted off of the surfaceless, bottomless eyes of the anthropoid moon—eyes like pools into which a visual diver could spelunk without ever knowing when or where he had entered, only certain of his entry because of the virtual, airtight caress of the delicate ocular texture that enveloped his body and left behind a film of pupil residue. Upon its return from the swelling plumes of galactic, spiritual mist, all light energy solidified into evil chemical matter in the Wheel of Consequence, which floated loyally into terrestrial Kambu's domain.

Kambu merely beckoned towards the Faustian device, and Krüstof knew immediately that the shaman would not grant him the convenience of spinning the wheel for him. Reluctantly, but deciding that he was already too far into this magical agreement to back out and appear a coward, the Chancellor plucked the lever with an audible and visible Krüsto-gulp. One by one, the braking nipple clicked across each spoke in the malevolent wheel. After exactly one eternity of scrutiny, the wheel finally rolled to a halt on "Birth 1,000 Spiders." Obviously displeased, Kambu blatantly extended one spindly finger and flicked the wheel again with a bulbous tip. The spokes clicked once more and came to rest on a much more ominous fate: "Auditory Dragon."

Clearly satisfied by this far superior retribution, Kambu delicately framed Krüstof's cranium and jowls with his gray, ethereal hands. He pulled the dandruffy meatball tight against his lips and let slip into the punished ear a blood-curdling ghost wail. The haunting shriek echoed permanently within Krüstof's acoustic sphere, punching the walls with pointed, concussive fists of discordant intensity. Krüstof fell to his knees and clasped his claws over his condemned ears. His stumpy neck writhed like a severed worm boiling dry in the relentless sun. Krüstof finally set his bloodshot, tired eyes on those of the preferable Kambu, who was clapping away in delight at having released a deafening beast-spirit from the overcrowded caverns of his cursed mind. Permanently, the immortal wyvern thrashed the silent gardens of the thenceforth forever spooked Krüstof's aural sanctuary, never again to grant him a moment's peace, and the Chancellor had earned one favor...

"OKAY," Krüstof roared over the thunderous, bit-crushed phantom howl that exploded within his head with an amplitude that exceeded the capacity of his temporal generators. "NOW KILL THE SLIMY ONE, PLEASE, IMPERATOR INCUBUS." Every word increased in volume, for the internal clangor of his punishment drowned out even the sound of his own voice, and he was unsure whether he was being too quiet.

Though slightly annoyed and wishing to enjoy Krüstof's anguish for a few moments more, Kambu remained faithful to his promise so as not to disturb the elemental balance of this ephemeral universe. From deep within his esophagus, Kambu retrieved a growling tokoloshe who dripped with globs of magical saliva. This was a being that Kambu had long since coaxed into

63

existence using a complex summoning ritual and that he had patiently stored in his stomach for precisely the correct moment: now. As Kambu raised his wrinkled, crumbling hand and paralyzed Ślimak mid-stride, the tokoloshe ripped a stubbed tooth from its white, dangling gums and prepared to spend hours stabbing Ślimak to death, practicing its swordsmanship with meek little swings of the dental blade and energetic grunts of pure excitation. But the impatient shaman had bugs to eat, and he quickly grew tired of the tokoloshe's insipid and ineffective attack maneuvers, which barely broke Ślimak's rocky skin. Even my brother himself yawned as he floated, immobilized and unafraid of the furious demon before him. Accessing the passcode servers for the time dimension, Kambu simply touched his whiz-stick to his tongue and whispered into it in muddled spells the command of chronological acceleration. For good measure, he also doubled the size of the tokoloshe and gave Ślimak embarrassing bunny ears. The two figures before him began frantically rushing through time, and the tokoloshe finally succeeded in slicing through Ślimak's chest plate without a trace of remorse or intention of relenting anytime soon, his arm still shanking the unfolding torso with the same mechanical frequency.

As my brother looked into the eyes of his taker, he whispered sour nothings, cursing Krüstof and the province to a horrendous fate, swearing vengeance. Kambu turned to a corpse at his foot and initiated the ancient ritual that would conjure the dreaded tokoloshe by shimmying his fingers between the tissues surrounding the skull and extracting the patient's brain from the nasal opening, along with several secret steps in the sorcerial process that no mortal could ever perceive due to their resonance on a psychic frequency beyond the absolute threshold of man. Punching out one of the corpse's eyeballs, out squirmed a wet, hairy tokoloshe baby, glistening with afterbirth and a thick coat of the man's blistered blood. The shaman carefully picked up and swallowed the beast that the ritual produced and sent it back in time to before he removed it from his throat. With a final thrust of the hand and pulsation of the fingers, Kambu uncaringly released Ślimak's body to the maggots, feeding them heartily as they chomped his tough protein. My brother died in the arms of evil, at the hand of the Devil, and by the acquiescent supervision of the almighty Beyond.

Uncle Rocco finished his routine with an exhausted look on his sweating face. I kicked him in the jaw and apologized, noticing the instant bruising on my ruined foot.

"You are a rock!" I realized. It appeared that I had accidentally drawn a face upon this stone with a marker and called it "uncle" for all three years of my life.

"Yes," Rocco responded. Screaming in terror, I sprinted to my bungalow and took refuge beneath the floorboards.

10: CRIMINAL DAWN

As I snuggled in the splinters and dust, the events of my childhood perturbed my throbbing mind, due partially to my emotional attachment to the figures I lost, and, more importantly, to my sense of helplessness at their demise; I had no means of rebellion and nothing to allow me any advantage over my nautical oppressor.

But alleviation finally met my impotent circumstances; just then, as one particularly sedimented breath contaminated my lungs with sand, three slow knocks flapped against my door, and I shimmied my way out from beneath the planks to answer. Pap Pap growled groggily, but I stuffed his mouth with cloth, and he suckled away, intrigued by the motley tastes of sweat and skin. I peered through the peep-hole, but when I remembered that the hole through which I pretended to look was drawn in crayon on the bare wood, I turned the knob, and the door fell flat to the ground off of its hinges. A robed man stood on my doorstep, his stringy white hair sailing in the stinging wind, his one arm sagging lankily down his waist. I could not see his face, for his cloak shadowed him into permanent darkness. He whispered into my dry ear with contrastingly moist lips.

"The fire grows," he breathed, bones wailing in agony. I sympathized with each individual skeletum on a spiritual level, offering my most dewy condolences. They suffered on, emotionally neglected by their biological liege lord who neither limped nor winced in acknowledgment of his raging ailments. I steamed cranially with resultant questions and complaints (for his breath stank of death and sorrow), but he had already turned, and as he trudged away, I could not see his feet, for, I assumed, his robe must have been too long.

I found that my hands caressed a brimy manuscript which weighed painfully on my cracking fingers whose inadequate bones failed miserably to support the 'nuscript's chulchritude. After silently thanking the Robed Man for his gift, I creaked open the rough leather cover, and a spout of dust and hair coated my face before absorbing my facial sweat like a parched sponge. The penmanship within was childlike and embarrassing, and on the cover two simple words beckoned me to read on: "My Struggle." Underneath was inscribed a name that wrenched a gasp from my astonished lungs; the manuscript's author was Krüstof.

"Written," however, proved inaccurate terminology. In fact, only one of the six hundred thousand pages had been tainted by Krüstof's ink, and on it suffered an unfinished diary entry, sagging and bleeding as would an infant born after only partial completion as a legless idiot. Obviously contrived by hired writing experts and not by the simple-minded Chancellor himself, it read as follows:

"I should never have entered The Yard. My grandfather had been a ferocious fighter, a perfect fit for the confrontations The Yard entailed, and for his son, my father, he had similar expectations. But my cowardish fathe suffered unbridled humiliation at the hands of Colimunda-Spander, the marauding bandit duo who lived typically unchallenged in The Yard after proving their macho-status over hundreds of years of victory in battle. My arrogant grandfather foolishly thought them worn and rusty, and he knew that if my father could defeat them, he would instantly be regarded as a threat not to

be confronted by other Yarddwellers. But father had no fighting experience as a two-month-old, and Colimunda-Spander laughed triumphantly as they swatted off the babe into a tearful, shamed refuge to The Darkroom, where all losers lived before I dismantled the olden system and established the Maggopolis of the present. Father lived [indecipherable squiggles] The Darkroom, and there I was born. No Roomler had ever ventured into the blinding tension of the temperamental outside, until [smudged area] and I exited, instantly fainting as the freshness of The Yard overwhelmed my underdeveloped senses. The Yarddwellers angrily circled me [penmanship lacking], but I screamed and peed, and they hesitated to pounce. I squealed and bled, and some weaker offensive-types backed away. They had never seen a Roomler, nor I one of their kind, and astonishment at the contrasting appearances made itself obvious from both ends. I found them oddly dry, and hard on the outside. They were dark people, but not because of an inkcoat, and they seemed painful to touch. I bellowed in rage, and I informed them that I sought an opponent to prove my belonging in the confrontational Yard. Many children were summoned by their fathers, who saw me as a weak opponent through which their children could prove their dominance. But I refused all, requesting specifically the formidable Colimunda-Spander, thinking of my father and the vengeance I would take. A hush came over the crowd, and one by one they turned to face their undeniable apex, several of them grinning in anticipation of the gory spectacle they would witness, hoping they could get their hands on some of the scraps. The bandit(s) had been sleeping and awoke flustered, confused that such a weird thing would challenge them. The lumbering Colimunda *seethed blue steam from its gums and rolled to allow pockets of smelly gas to wriggle out of its fat, while Spander grinned as he sharpened his formidable claws and picked the bones from his teeth. Colimunda groaned as Spander tugged its hairs as reins, guiding the beast across the field as lesser fighters cleared the way for their superior(s). The bloodthirsty duo, towering fifteen feet into the sky, plopped itself before me, completely oblivious to the grim truth: that particular sleep from which they had awoken would be their last before the eternal slumber I induced with my greased fist and scissoring teeth, what would mark my acceptance into the belligerent world of The Yard...."*

I hated the Robed Man for raising my hopes only to give me such a useless gift as this manuscript. Moron. I decided, however, that regardless of the writing's actual contents, the symbolism of the Robed Man's gift did carry significance. Even if I learned nothing of importance from Krüstof's most personal inner machinations, I knew with absolute certainty that the delivery of this "diary" (hahaha) was a sign from the heavens that my rebellion had completely developed and awaited the first ovulation. I pounded the floorboards in anger, screaming for my life, wallowing in self pity. I thought of my fathers. Of my brother, the first rebellious spirit I ever encountered, though I happily say he was not the last. Their deaths were not in vain, for on that day their stories sparked my rebellion. Krüstof would pay; reckoning awaited.

I am Larwa. Larwa Chłopak. Early into my life I understood, unlike my ignorant peers, that our conditions of existence were intolerable and would not have been acceptable prior to the war. Indeed, our circumstances were barely primitive at best, and life

69

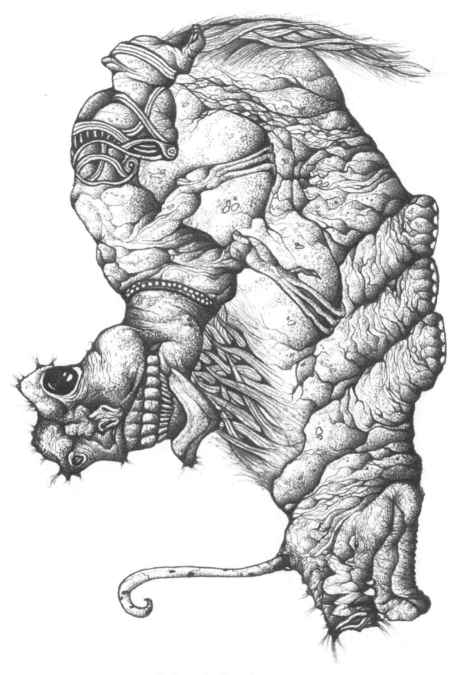

Colimunda-Spander

under such oppressive rule was so horrid that death evoked mouthwatering desire upon life's sorry residents. I wept for my people—the forgotten laborers of Grunty Kraba—and their grueling ignorance inspired my anger.

The roar of a biological megaphone interrupted my grieving. Through the blur of my tears, mopping up the blood that was inexplicably pouring from my mouth, I located Krüstof himself wandering the farms, screeching self-praising propaganda through an unfortunate sacrifice; the Chancellor screamed into the ear of a government official whose open mouth amplified the bellow. The advertisement had likely been occurring for a few hours now, for the official had long ago died from auditory destruction.

"I am your president! I am your king! I am pretty! I am tall! And I smell good, and also I am smart, and funny…" The Chancellor paused as he thought of more of his characteristics. The Chancellor was everything. He was nothing. He was them, and he was us. He was you, and he was me. He was the writing on the wall, the strings that pulled the men on whom he stepped.

My rage could not be contained. How dare he? How dare he take so much from me and refuse to allow me a moment's solitude? I severed all ties to righteousness, destroyed all chance of governmental forgiveness, and ascertained my future as an outlaw, exiled for life, through one hot-headed action: I flatulated, rectally, in Krüstof's vicinity and presence. Krüstof quickly removed his nose and threw it as far as possible: one meter.

"Puppeteer, tug on my string and keep me above this cloud! Who has violated my legislation?" he inquired (It was forbidden, of course, to expel any gas, excretory or otherwise, within sniffing distance of the almighty Crab-O.)

I stood red-faced before the Chancellor in the green vapor of my production.

"You? Boy?" he chortled. I managed a meek, frightened nod beneath his intimidating shadow. "I see the fires in your pupils. Have I taken something from you? Your family? Your friends? Yes… I see your fires. You are the boy of fire! I was a boy of something different. But I will not tease you for what you are. Instead, I will take everything you have ever loved. Do you understand? Any person, place, thing, idea, thought, concept you have ever enjoyed—I will devour them all. To your fire, I will be… wet." He smiled.

Flatulence: an easy infraction to commit, but an infraction that would mark the dawn of the long rivalry that would perpetuate throughout the entire remaining lives of both myself and Krüstof, for never would our souls find peace with one another.

11: SCOURGE OF THE CRAB

Amassing the criminal momentum I created with my first ever violation, I took to crime, mainly because it made me seem cool among the popular trio of Grunty Kraba, composed of an elderly pumpkin spirit I affectionately named "Jank," oSpondylus Rink, a distinguished and beloved aristocrat, and Kambu, the shaman. Though they all believed firmly in the domineering righteousness of the law, they somehow lauded my lack of legal complacency not as disregard for the common good but rather as determined attention to the force of style; whether or not they liked it, some foreign hiplord had recently ruled that petty crimes were in, and while none of them dared prioritize the higher authority of fashion for fear of governmental punishment, they admired my hierarchically correct adherence to funk above law. I began with minor grievances to the irritable Chancellor: eating federal dirt, punching concrete, touching my head in front of Krüstof himself, speaking. Few could boast enough muscle to escape for more than a few feet after committing such insignificant but readily punishable offenses, but my semi-developed legs provided me this crucial advantage, meaning that the squadron of decrepit policemen sent to find me after each infraction always succeeded only in blasting their asses out in trying to capture as physically "fit" a lad as myself.

My refuge took the form of a friendly giant: Tarfüglio. His seemingly cancerous and unreasonably gargantuan fingers plucked my comparatively miniscule self from the dangers of Gruntian territory to the safety of the earth's second floor, where I would observe the bleak ground below from his sloshy chest. Giant beings inhabited that world—amoebic creatures built for sheer mass over

73

intelligence or efficiency—and they remained afloat by constantly grabbing one another and throwing themselves back into the sky, what resulted in one confusing and grossly tactile celestial heap of limbs and fat. The thousand-foot-tall beasts towered on a plane hundreds of miles above the dirt on which we treaded, and their stalactite chins often dripped fatty bulbs that would sometimes fortunately land on their feet to which they would attach like biological stalagmites, but would other times be lost to the malnourished world of grounded mortals; such fat slabs rained destructively upon the village, but although they ravaged our straw and clay households, they came as welcome signs of a merciful Almighty, for we feasted heartily upon the flesh droplets of the above giants. Tarfüglio was one such being, and one who I could almost lovingly deem my friend, only lacking such a distinction because of my overwhelming fear of so physically powerful an organism. He rejoiced endlessly at the tales of my crimes for which he begged.

"Do Lorwa, tell moe moer! Tell moe abot yor baed daeds yaou ded! Haehoaeheh!" he loudly messed, teeth falling from his crusted gums, eyes trickling down his bubbling cheek.

"Um… Today, I stepped on some special rock… Krüstof was mad," I stammered frightfully, Tarfüglio's booming breath dwarfing my miniscule own.

At this Tarfüglio wildly roared. "BAAAAUGH! YAOU MAED THE PYUNY CREB MAEN ANGERY LOIK AN IDYOET! AAAAUUEHAEHAEO!" His neck veins popped and leaked chunky ink, and his exploding eyes bulged and vomited in untamed amusement. Drule overflowed his maw and spilled into open pores on his greasy chest. He grabbed his own feet and slung them mightily over his head, throwing himself and me back to the top of the floating meat conglomeration, for our freefall had begun to grow worryingly magnitudinous.

Encouraged, I continued: "And I pinched a big stick that Krüstof liked. And then–"

"YAOU DED WHAET TAO HEM? AAAHAEHAEUHEAOEUH! LORWA IS YAES!" I warned him to keep his voice down, now beginning to worry that the Chancellor would catch wind of my residence and hurt my colossal acquaintance. Catching his breath and massaging his pulsing arteries to control the excessive inkflow, Tarfüglio muddily panted and fortunately remembered to grab a fellow giant's leg and use the resultant leverage to throw himself back into the heavens. He sporadically wheezed with bewildered eyes and glistening head sweat, but did his best to control himself for my sake more than his. I did love him, and I relished napping against his fleshy cancerous nubs, wrapping his folds around my back and drifting into sleep when I could squeeze enough sand out of my eyes to force them shut.

On that day, as I scraped his belly grease out of my hair after my comfortable awakening, I bid Tarfüglio an emotional goodbye before leaping back down to the earth. I brushed my teeth with the frigid air as I rested against the pointed blanket of drag at terminal velocity. By the time the planet cared enough about me to remember to pull me down, the night had begun to reluctantly give way to the day, and the ominous bells prepared to signal to all infants that a new morning had presented itself for the dedication of self to the service of the sector.

12: In Negligence She Thrives

The pale sun ascended but did not illuminate the foamy clouds as it rose like a zombified corpse, instead leaving the task of visible exuberance to the air itself. The morning sky was a splash of color as diverse as a painter's palette, and the gaseous bodies seemed to speak amongst themselves in an elemental tongue, whispering wisps of wind that tangled around each other and purred. Scattered tufts of clouds glowed a soft lavender, then mellowed into a deeper purple, soon to become more vibrant, reflecting their own orange light like a gently flickering flame. The fiery yellow rays blended onto the barren fields and woods—an odd contrast of color. Indeed, a spectacular beauty characterized that morning; nature seemed to have given me her blessing as I commuted through the fields to take count on the harvest and make inspections.

The melancholy reminder, however, soon manifested that I still called a cruel world home; rotting corpses of deer and rodent lay strewn about the fields, displayed in barbarically mangled poses as their flesh withered, and chemicals emitted a low hiss as they bubbled away at their emaciated innards. The maggots could be heard within, making moist sounds like the sloppy lip-smacking of an elderly man with swollen salivary glands and a mouthful of spit. I cringed and shuddered a bit as I trudged past, the bitter wind lashing at my face like icy whips, blistering my rosy cheeks. Winter's crisp, subzero breath frosted my path, tempting me to flee for a warm shelter, but hypocritically whispering pleas for my continuation. "Onward," she daringly breathed.

77

The wolves are real. They are in the stories I have heard. They are here and now. They are every disturbance of the leaves, every shadow in the periphery. However, they are not fools that I have eluded in the past. I have seen that some men are rhatts, others: dogs. But from no man's face has a wolf ever looked upon me. Never has my life been poised upon the hunger and certainty of a beast that would rip me apart with its own teeth. I am the narrow trail. The wolves are all that hide in the palm of the forest.

I proceeded cautiously, quivering and twitching as I imagined the malnourished wolves of the forest abruptly growling and briskly lunging into my fetal carcass, tearing away at me with their powerful claws. I hunched over furtively to pass stealthily through the thick of the wood until I reached the clearing undisturbed.

Plastic tarps covered every individual hay bale, like a feeble, caring mother of the myths tucking in her grassy wee-ones for their final snore. The plastic cover shielded from the weather's roughness and also protected the synthesized nutrients injected into the hay from leaching. The rows of bales extended seemingly without end. At first, the cool breeze slowly wafted the subtle aroma of rodent droppings into my sodden nostrils, tickling my nasal hairs and gently rocking my boogers. But very quickly, the smell evolved into a more putrid fragrance, one that enacted a rude awakening upon my mucus. "My poor boogies!" I thought. After being lovingly stirred by the motherly touch of the original scent, they had abruptly experienced the burning sensation of glaring light as the fatherly incarnation of the fecal odor opened the blinds with merciless disregard, releasing the full potential of the poopish rank and bursting my mucus membranes.

I reached into my satchel with one hand to withdraw my clipboard and pinched my nose tight with the other as I mildly wheezed, almost spiraling myself into a coughing fit. It was my third winter in charge of the periodical check-ups on the town's food supply. We could not survive solely off of the stale maggot crisps; Gruntian diet could only be completed with hay cuisine such as hay soup or other hay eats, with hay, yes, in them. The sulfuric scent of the methane scorched the lush, fleshy cushioning of my nasal passages and burned the outer ridges of my nostrils despite my efforts to pinch the odor out, furthering my previous nasal injuries, and blood trickled down to my sandy lips. Distracted in thought, I carelessly overlooked the threatening presence of a Siberian Snow Puffer that had taken refuge under the first tarp I had lifted to inspect.

It only took a second's glance to identify, although I barely caught a glimpse. I knew exactly what it looked like; its image vividly flashed in my mind–the bright verdant eyes striped with vicious black slits, the thin, pearly fangs, the glossy white finish to its thickly padded scales. The snake quickly became a blur as I jolted backwards, disoriented, dazed, and although I understood my circumstances exactly, a strange primitive blankness erased my ability to cognize manually. But the sporadic rattling of its coiled tail plunged me back into reality, and I collapsed into my defensive position and scrambled about on my hands and knees in attempt to distance myself from my serpentine foe. Its forked tongue flicked my forehead as its eyes fixated on my fearful face. I stumbled into an upright position and scurried away, often tripping as I pitifully scampered towards the village, tears streaming as I moaned.

79

My heart pounded against my ribcage, roaring like a mechanical beast as I tore through the thick foliage in the forest. I hurdled brambles and vaulted the underbrush as my heart's deafening surge pounded in my eardrums, drowning out all other sound. I posted myself upright against a hearty oak and then slowly slouched into a seated position, attempting to recollect myself. My heartbeat gradually decelerated, and my thin, stringy muscles unclenched their crushing embrace upon my bones, easing into a relaxed state as my respiration normalized.

I abandoned my day's labor to escape the fanged devil. This, however, was no excuse to foolishly offer Krüstof, who, like the omnipresent Chancellor he was, manifested himself from inside of my mouth. I coughed him out, and after a moment's rolling about the dirt to soak off my saliva, he presented an outstretched claw into which he demanded I place my handwritten evaluation.

"You aren't about to fart again, are you?" Krüstof nervously posed.

"No. Sorry." Awkward!

A lengthy pause of anxious foot-shuffling.

"Well, boy? Have you your papers?"

"That... yes." Whipping out my pen and performance evaluation form, I decided to avoid my predicament by checking the box labeled "field cleared and prepared for human consumption." But just then, as I prepared to hand the Chancellor my clipboard, I hesitated; it occurred to me that the shit smell that attacked me in the hay bales was potentially the scattered feces of a rhatt infestation. I only then recalled that I had marked the "no rodent infestation" box on my clipboard without actually even laying eyes upon the hay bales. But never had I encountered any complications in the past; why would I this winter? I rolled those laughing bones and decided to hand over the clipboard to Krüstof. Done and done!

I could not have been more wrong, for a formidable infestation that I had overlooked fermented in the hay storage fields that winter–an infestation of creatures far more pernicious than rhatts.

13: THOSE VALIANT NIGHTMARES

The pestilence made itself known to me through the medium of pediatric destruction. Two days had rolled by since the incident with the dreaded Snow Puffer, and its memory continued to traumatize my infantile brain. My fascination with my toes ran rampant through my consciousness at the time, and I aerated them happily with heartfelt laughter. I loved their texture, the dank gook that sweated out of their bloated pores, the lint trapped betwixt my nail and skin, yet to be roughened by the callouses of labor. I wept joyfully as their wet stench intrusively marched into my nostrils, and each time I wiggled one toe, a new, previously undiscovered odor bubble would emerge, noisily creeping up the thick air. "Galoonkaloonkoonk!" the bubbles blupped. Ah, how blissful my days were when my toes were still soft! It would not be long before I could not even touch my digits without my hands bleeding, for scars and blisters made them jagged and scraped through with serrated skin. Soon, confident that all stank bubbles had blackishly risen into the great Beyond, I rested my weary spine upon my front porch, puncturing my supple skin with millions of moist splinters. This was normal. I dozed off in pain, but comforted by the thought of my peculiarly appealing toes.

A mist twirls from the metal belly of The Darkroom's chambers. Swirling steam spirals from the dungeon fog like a militia of ballerinas tearing the surface upon the damp draft with each thunderous pirouette. Emerging in crawl, first veiled in the settling dungeon steam, the prisoner is illuminated as beams flicker through the trees to pierce his shroud. In the strangeness of the bright sunshine I linger alone. Hotly, I blink like a mole at the sun. Curdled milk—my gelatin skin, cold ink—the web of blood frozen inside him. Out here, there is no night to divide the day. Land of eternal sun. The rays are intensely white and my pupils crinkle upon the dry film of my irises like the eyes of a dead fish drying on a beach. Vision fades and sharpens until my sight evaporates. My sagging eyelids crust inwards. The pains sting deeply like the searing cry of the cicada which now emulate the Sun's radiance in a ringing choir. "The children of the gods are not human," they seem to be screaming. I scuttle nervously because I know these bugs have stinky green scales. The haze of mold lingering in the humidity augments as the pit breathes. Hopes to slip from incarceration are suppressed by fears... It seems the familiarity of imprisonment keeps cool arms spread, waiting to cradle next, whoever be cast into its clutches. Perhaps I'd have to confide in the artificial company I found conveniently provided in the shelter of darkness. After all, who knew for sure whether The Yard still existed.

Rudely, my brief dream shattered by means of agony whose epicenter was none other than my blessed toes. I manually wrenched my eyelids apart to gather sight of this pain's source, but my dried pupils failed to provide an instant view of the culprit. Thus the pain continued, uninterrupted, for my coordination had yet to develop at my young age, and without my sight I was a useless creature incapable of doing anything other than puking to save my endangered body. Looking back at my foolishness in utter disappointment, any moderately intelligent child, or even beast for that matter, would have immediately thought to stand up and run away from the peril, or at least batted at their foot to injure and deter the assailant.

From the pestering at my feet, I concluded that some sort of living being was mangling my toes. It seemed to beat at them, shoving small sticks into their fat, which would envelop the sticks, leaving misshapen indents and craters speckling my phalanges like the moon's dotted surface. More annoyingly, some sort of wet noodle, drenched in a viscous glue, dragged over my still-developing epidermis, and when it was picked up, it tore chunks of skin off with it. My raw toes bled, and acidic gas bubbles manifested corrosively at their surfaces, gnawing further into my skin and snapping ligaments to weaken their attachment to my feet. The pain suddenly shifted from caustic decomposition to a strange tugging feeling. What could only be described as tweezers gripped my bloody, soft toes, gushing water and soggy tendons, and began to separate their bones from my foot. I tried desperately to stop this, for I loved my dactyls and knew finally my marauder's intent, but my feeble mind could not think to kick my attacker away. Skin cells, weakened by the noodle whips, opened a seam between the knuckle and base of the foot, slowly peeling deeper and reaching bone. One swift crack resonated into the air, and I suddenly lost control of my beloved footfingers as my muscle slid off my bone like tender rib meat from its rack.

No existing* words can authentically describe the empty feeling of incompleteness that emerges upon the removal of one's appendages. Though the mind fails to comprehend that its cells no longer have dominion over the removed structure, the eyes reluctantly affirm that the body lacks a once extant component, and the discrepancy between the two organs causes undeniable confusion in one's thoughts, especially those of an uncomprehending two year old boy. Fortunately, I was four. But wait; THIS IS STILL BAD.

My eyes regained usefulness just in time to catch a glimpse of my thief, wheeling a cart filled with my precious toes, as it retreated to its home in the hay, and I would never forget the mortifying sight.

It could only be considered a tiny person, but even this would be an inadequate classification, for its mutilations were multifarious and dramatic. His four stumpy arms clasped his creaky cart weakly, and it was now clear that these were the instruments of torture that had pulverized my toes, which now sat in the thief's little wheelbarrow. Those "arms" of his had no fingers, and so each handle was loosely wedged between a pair of his limbs. But apart from these appendages dangled two thick, lumpy, vestigial arms, neither of which retained the necessary nerve endings for movement. His solitary leg boinged like an oiled spring, muscular in some parts and yet dystrophic in others, and his brittle heart pumped steadily upon his head. A long, goopy tongue, which I soon realized was the glue-covered noodle I'd felt upon my foot, hung trailing from his circular lip, slathered in thick, adhesive saliva. The spawn of Chaos hobbled off with my toes, oinking and wheezing with its dilapidated accordion lungs, satisfied by its successful treachery.

My embryonic brain finally fit the pieces together. This fiend was a product of my own negligence; I knew then that my failure to inspect each bale had been an immense mistake. There was no

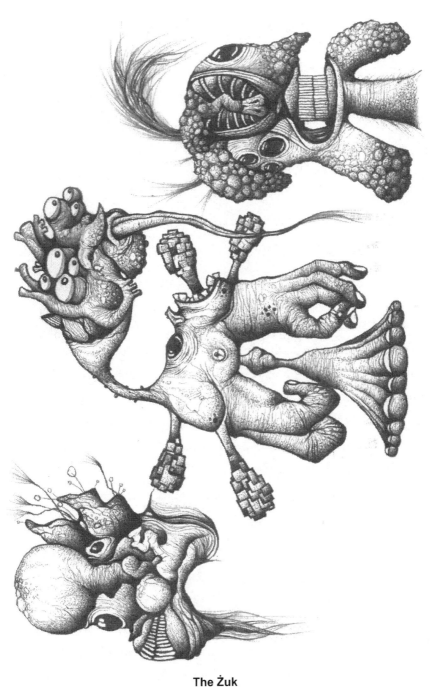

The Żuk

colony of rhatts in the hay. Something else existed there. They were arbitrarily known as the Żuk. A race of six inch tall interbred mutations, they preyed on beetles in crunchy, cacophonous feeding frenzies. Had I inspected the hay bales thoroughly, the infestation of beetles would have become clear to me and would have been easily eradicated. My carelessness had brought about the Żuk plague, for with an ample food source of overpopulated bugs, the beasts thrived in the damp hay chunks within which they found shelter. The ideal conditions for reproduction produced a population explosion upon the mini humanoids, whose numbers soon approached quadruple digits, and they proved themselves an undeniably vexatious source of mischief.

Rather than fear the Siberian Snow Puffer, which I originally assumed would be their natural predator, the Żuk revered the beast, worshipping it righteously through songs and scriptures dedicated to their reptilian idol. The fiend was kind to them, taking only one sacrifice daily, which the Żuk saw as a fair compromise for what they perceived as bottomless benevolence from their God, who, they reasoned, could easily destroy their entire species but instead allowed their fruitful existence.

Krüstof's inspectors, most of us still confined to the inconvenience of diapers, left him unimpressed, and he solely blamed us for this Żuk scourge, ordering the execution of all hay bale sleuths not long after the initial outbreak. Krüstof had no sympathy for us children; he sincerely believed we deserved death for our inability to follow what he perceived as the simplest of orders. Our sole task was to prevent these outbreaks, and our failure kindled his infamous rage. It is for this reason that Father B16 received a letter with my death sentence. The Chancellor himself squirmed out from the giant envelope and collapsed onto the floor.

"Your boy has offended my honor. I will kill him now. It's the right thing to do," Krüstof asserted. "The Executioner will arrive promptly at noon tomorrow. He's sweet. You'll take a fancy to him." Krüstof boinked his head to each shoulder in a glorphish manner and winked profusely. Forefingers on temples, he gave a sharp raspberry with his dark, stubby tongue and zapped Father B16 with his mind. Fortuitously, my fathe was not zapped into the void.

Krüstof had been entirely truthful, for not only did the Executioner knock on the Chłopak door at exactly 12:00, but Father B16 also strangely admired the man who would soon kill his son; my supposed doombringer had an inviting aura to him, one that pacified even my fear in facing his custom-engraved battle axe—the sweetest blade I ever did see.

"Sorry I must do this, boy," he began. "What a shame that Krüstof took a dislike to you. You had promise. May your soul be salvaged," his raspy, pained voice echoed. And as he wielded his instrument of murder, my soft eyes, compensating for my wordless tongue, delivered him a look of reassurance and understanding that seemed to say "I forgive you." A single tear trickled down his bristly cheek, but he was bound to his labor, determined to accomplish the task to which he had been assigned. He rose his blade.

Suddenly, the hay rumbled and stirred with life. A teeming ecosystem of Żuk emerged, chanting unintelligible rhymes and poems while facing the Executioner's confused peep. They performed spiritual rituals, summoning the Siberian Snow Puffer from the depths of the earth. It leapt briskly at the Executioner, and, following the will of its worshipping subjects, sunk its fangs into his lean neck. He seemed to be somehow relieved, satisfied that this creature had taken his life before he had been forced to take that of the innocent child before him, and he appeared confident that his spirit would ascend into the glorious above on which he had waited so patiently–the sweet luxury that was release from his grim life in Grunty Kraba. His veins decayed as the poison spread, popping blood vessels and disintegrating organs, until the spark of life fell from his cold lips, leaving only black oil to spurt from his collapsed throat. As his misery culminated into death and the Puppeteer snipped his string, I caught his gaze, and I wept softly for his departure. I believe he might have been the last "good" guy left.

The Żuk platoon dutifully saluted me. I owed them an unrepayable debt, for they had willed their God into saving my life. But their silent eyes told me there was no need to feel indebted. I had granted them their lives by failing to exterminate the beetles, and they merely returned that favor by preserving mine. I addressed their salute with one of my own, proud to have become acquainted with such a rationally reciprocal species. Sympathizing with my obvious desire to recount my escape of the Chancellor's wrath to a certain companion, the Żuk tolerated one more favor that I requested:

Hacking into their cyberkinetic hive mind, I willed the swarm to lump their individual entities into one organic staircase spiralling towards the heavens. But I remained unconvinced that their biological architecture would be anything but precarious, despite their unnatural athleticism due to years of gymnastics training. Indeed, for years the Żuk had relentlessly rehearsed assembling

89

themselves into intricate pyramids designed by the stonemasons and choreographed by olympic gymnast Mark Splitz. Though their cheerleading team was world renowned as the most accomplished and unsettlingly limber of all time, they still yearned to break the boundaries of human athleticism by executing a perfect No Pants Space Staircase Stance–a mythical pose long considered impossible on the planet Earth. Tumbling experts and quantum physicists worldwide performed multiple anatomy studies with parent signatures disproving the possibility of any team successfully performing so complex a structure. They produced supply and demand graphs indicating a constant zero supply and infinite demand, leading to an inconceivably high equilibrium price: death. But no matter how many reports from ex. marine biologists or ancient Greek astronomers estimated at least one hundred irreparable instances of bone destruction and brain decay, their estimations were mere bottles of liquor smashed against the heads of Żuk so drunk on their passions that they remained entirely unfazed by calculation. A panel of distinguished cheerleading judges gathered to evaluate their performance as the hoard assembled before me. I observed as each Żuk bled sandy sweat from its furrowed brow, which quivered in the silent meditation of a concentration conjoined in a collective nucleus formed in the center of the pulsating mass. Up went the scoreboards, one by one. Perfect tens across the board. The mothers of the victors choked on each other's stinky tears, overwhelmed in witnessing the holy transformation of the boys not only into men, but into legends forever preserved in stone.

The Żuk seemed to entreat me to ascend their masterpiece, and I did not disappoint, hoisting myself upward with the limbs that formed the rails and treading on their faces to enter the realm of Tarfüglio. But growing weary of the structural integrity and skeptical of the judges' credentials, I raced back down, worried that the arrangement of bodies would be too unstable for prolonged scaling. I swiped the scoreboard from the limp fingers of the center judge and smashed it over his skull. I scanned over the notes on the clipboard of the judge to my right. Utterly unimpressed, I snatched his pencil mid-scribble and pierced the sphincter of his ear. I snapped another clipboard in two with one powerful kick, and I fashioned a makeshift crucifix from the two wooden pieces. As the final judge attempted to scurry away, I gently bit him by the scruff of his neck and waddled the pup back. Returning to the cross, firmly planted upside down in the soil, I crucified him like the devil he was, feet in the air, hair hanging into the blazing pits of Hell.

I tickled my holster and swiftly quick-drew my Argon Beam Rapid Blaster ®, taking aim before I even turned to face the Żuk escalator.

"You… Ar-gone!" I exclaimed with a smirk. I unloaded my entire magazine of lethal zaps unto the tower, melting the Żuk momentarily before their molten flesh solidified into one hunk of electrified meat. I felt the odor sludge its way through my nostrils and sharply inflate up into the back of my skull, leaving behind wet globs that rolled out and stung my lip. It slipped through the cracks of my bone and trickled onto the back of my tongue, where it collected and fizzed like battery acid before sliding down my throat like fat, putrid ghost cheese.

91

Reverting to infantile stair-scaling stratagem, I accessed my quadrupedalism and bounded onto the caramelized mass. I found my slippery hike up the slope to be much akin to a trek through fresh mud; my boots, which grew heavy as globs of doughy skin collected on the outsole, sunk into the chunky puddles of hot epidermis. After a few hours of this grueling trudge, Tarfüglio's booming howls rejuvenated the stride of my prance. With a renewed vigor, I crawled my way to the top and rejoiced in seeing my gargantuan companion once more. I belly-flopped into the refuge of my favorite mattress–Tarfüglio.

"LORWORM! YAOU DONE COME PAEYD A VISIT FOR MOE?" Fragments of his shredded vocal cords ensconced themselves in my forehead, and I was soothed by the acupuncture of his melodic voice, which fingered the wrinkles in my face and massaged my muscles into the delicate domain of bliss. "Do tell moe WHAT YOU DED? AAHUAEHUUH! WHAT DED YAOU DO TO THE LITTLE CRAB GUY?"

"Well, this time–"

"Hueheh…"

"Well, I–"

"HueaAAH! HUAAH!"

"I didn't make sure–"

"WHAT? YAOU DEDENT, AHUEH, YAOU DED WHAT TO… HUAAHUEHAH!"

I decided that attempting to explain my misdeeds to him would be a futile pursuit and instead simply allowed him to spew foamy spit from his maw as parasitic laughter overtook his bodily function. His pupils exploded and painted his inflated eyes a deep, frozen obsidian, and his violent inhaling vacuumed his elephantine nose into his mouth and down his throat. I frolicked through the forestial groves defined by his stomach hairs, swinging around on the thick, greasy follicles like on monkey bars, while he wrenched his snout from his esophagus and punched himself in the face to forcibly mollify his vocal clangor. A warm smile trickled across my lips as I finally settled myself within the velvety blanketing of his belly-button lint. There, cozy and safe, I contemplated the four years during which I had existed. Four years—no more. And yet I had been condemned to sorrow that would last any other man a lifetime. Misery lived—still lives—in society. It breathes our anxiety. Imbibes our submission. And we were all pawns in the grand, inescapable machine, puppets of the crooked crustacean apprentice of the ambiguvalent, omniscient master. They would stifle us with rules and stone, and we would forget that we were born of the wild that would one day return to reclaim its throne.

But it was no time for tears; each corrosive drop would eat away at Tarfüglio's skin. That night, I decided, I would forget. Tomorrow would return my despair, but that rest would be one of rare indulgence.

14: FLIGHT OF THE VALKYRIES

Stirring me in the wee hours of the winter morn, an eerie, wooden creaking echoed within the chasms of my ear canal, gently rapping against the leathery membrane of my eardrum like a nervous percussionist cautiously tapping his drum. I sat erect in my poorly constructed sleeping quarters, noting the gaping hole in my ceiling suggesting that Tarfüglio had plunged his arm down from the heavens and through my roof to place me carefully into my bungalow. A collection of carelessly strewn hides and threadbare cloth in a huddled corner served as my bed on which I wept every day upon returning from the commercial maggot farms. I sluggishly extended my arms and planted them in front of my knees, mobilizing myself on all fours. I scuttled over to the wall facing the "road" in a hurried scurry, and I gingerly pressed my face into the rotting wood, squinting my eyes through a split in one of the spruce logs to serve as my viewing window.

I identified the source of the rhythmic creaking as the musical labors of a wooden-spoked wheel bearing the weight of a covered wagon. Two sickly horses, rib cages exposed, slowly wobbled into our village with their heads hung low, acquiescently pulling the wagon, the cotton cover of which was tattered and faded. A hooded figure veered the wooden cart off the dirt roads and onto the grassy stretch across the front of my abode. The robed conductor of the horse-powered vehicle briefly scanned down my shack with an expert ocular patdown and abruptly halted the ill mares, then dismounted from his conducting stance. He circled to the rear and proceeded to roll his corpulent kinder out from the wagon.

94

The mysterious man and his plump kin approached my wretched den—my molded shelter. The door flung open with the fatty's hefty shove, and the powerful push nearly ripped the door off its hinges again; the foundations shuddered and the wooden house nearly collapsed with the immense blast of raw power. I quivered with a magnificent start as the two shadows entered through the door frame. Their bodies were hard silhouettes cast in front of the rising sun as it made its commute to the heights of the forever stretching sky. They drifted to the corner to settle their baggage, and as they swayed from the direct light, their bodies were displayed in full color.

Before introducing himself, the conductor unsheathed a sword and plunged it into the heart of my infant brother, discarding the weapon afterwards. He reached for a parchment concealed in his robe pocket and preluded by explaining that after a maggot mauling dispatched my most recent father, he—the stranger—was entitled to my father's property.

"I am your uncle," he claimed, jerking his chubby son over with a tug of a leash. "You may call me Uncle Chadwick, and this is my sweety boy, Yuelfrik."

"I believe you," I replied. Instantly I accepted his allegation of blood-relation, for his presence enchantingly welcomed and warmed. He was a muscular man, boasting rectangular, thick shoulders and stocky arms. His temples were dense bulks lined with thick, bushy brows, and they shifted quizzically as he scoured the land for place to sow his grain. As a solid grandeur, he reaped harvest faster than any other—a classic demonstration of the ideal communist workhorse. But he was kind to me and fed me wheat

95

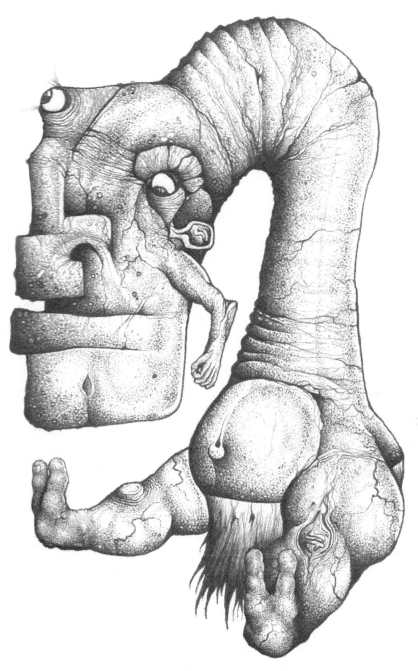

Yuelfrik

soup, often picking the bats out of my hair as I slurped. Unfortunately, his worsening illness jeopardized my growing fondness of the man; it appeared that he aged at an alarming rate, and what age-suggesting features would take a healthy man a year to develop, my uncle would experience in only the span of a few days.

There were many more children in our village that year—a surplus selection of work hands. Such an influx in labor seldom occurred, and maggot duties typified our usual assignments. Breeders overcrowded the farms, so Krüstof invented and subsequently assigned various arbitrary positions to convey the illusion of order. My cousin Yuelfrik—Uncle Chadwick's son—and I were enlisted to guard duties.

We kept watchful eyes cast on the skirmishes, and every day, Yuelfrik hauled himself and his wiggling belly up a tree to mount his post. He would always scale the same pine. His meaty belly remained perpetually covered with scratches and rashes as the tree chafed his stomach. He climbed so far up the tree that we could not communicate by means of our weak tongues; we had no organized sign language, but instead an intricate system of suggestive hand gestures and interpretive maneuvers, so the correspondent to whom the signals were addressed could guess the transmission's intent with relative accuracy.

From the canopy's heights, Yuelfrik spotted a stream, snaking in and out of the forest's shady cover. He plucked a single feather from a bird that soared by him. Uncle Chadwick would glow with pride to know his son truly possessed the same handicraft as his father—handicraft that became blatantly evident as he unsheathed a knife that he had smithed with a straight razor and an antler fragment. He shaved a sheet of paper from the pine tree and then dipped the feather into his inky pupil. Then, he pronounced the consummation of pen and paper and sketched a route to the stream.

We spared no time, abandoning our posts to explore our findings. The rushing water hissed louder as we marched closer. We stood on a boulder that extended over the water, and the stream was wide and golden like honey. Otters floated on their backs, clam shells on their round bellies, and trout seemed to hover underneath the shady spots that the otters cast into the water. This liquid was unlike the mucky, clumpy bogwater we were forced to drink back home; it was crisp and delicate, reflecting clean, flexible beams of white light in an elastic dance against the pearly pebbles over which it flowed. Yuelfrik gleefully wrapped himself around me as he tackled me off the ledge, into the warm, sunlit stream below. We splashed around quite a bit until I momentarily retired to look around and absorb my surroundings, and as I made my observations, Yuelfrik began engineering some aquatic devices. From the river reed on the banks, he fashioned himself a snorkel, and with the water grass and the slippery algae on the stones, he created a tickle machine. Using his new crafts, he dipped under the visible depth and then tickled my feet as he surfaced. This stream must have eluded the grasp of Time, and it had certainly only stopped in Grunty Kraba for a brief sojourn, likely to make itself feel better about its own surroundings back home. As the boy in the days of old had hesitated to leave the carnival, fearing that it might not remain upon his return, soaking up each possible droplet of entertainment, so too did we thoroughly nourish ourselves in the young water, so bereft of the stain of degenerating longevity, suspecting that at any moment the stream might vanish.

We were enjoying our afternoon, but our fingers were inflating like prunes, and we had to rest from our swim. We strolled alongside the stream, inspecting the banter of the otters. My inattention to the ground ahead almost cost me a step into something rather unpleasant; my foot's foresight, however, sensed an unusual object in the short grass and denied my step forward. What lay in front of me appeared to be what I can only describe as a stone with skin. I sniffed at it as I knelt beside it, and it smelled not like a rock, but rather like an old, earthy decomposition. I met a certain reluctance with the root's tenacity in the ground, but it budged without too much of a tug. The underside was dusty and polished with pristine dirt, so I thought to scrub it in the stream to decrease its age by the transitive property (this science is beyond your comprehension). I dunked it in the water and scrubbed once, but, suddenly, it let out the cry of a baby! I cradled it just above the rippling water as it wailed. The root had a weird face, but before I could commit its features to memory, a furry pair of paws clawed the root from my hand. A dark otter king swam quickly away, and I saw the sparkle of his crown disappear into an underwater cave. The otters lazing on the surface swiped the shells off their bellies and dove after their king, all of them swarming into the same hole. I hoped I hadn't done something very wrong.

I thought we should perhaps utilize Yuelfrik's snorkel to retrieve the root baby, but Yuelfrik reminded me that we did not know anything with concerns to the nature of an otter king, and perhaps it was best

99

Root Baby

we left. A harmless accident, or a rightful source of the guilt I felt? I could not yet determine, but I suffered tremendously from anxiety, and I could tell Yuelfrik shared some of my worry. But as our concerns elapsed, perhaps in an effort to ease our nerves, Yuelfrik made random and frankly inopportune talk of his father. He explained to me that Chadwick was his third father, but he had an adeptness of inconspicuity that kept him in the shadows of Krüstof's wrath, and so Yuelfrik had lived with this man as his father for twelve long years—an unprecedented paternal era in Grunty Kraba.

Honestly, not to be rude, but at the moment, the statements merited exactly zero Care Points on my part, but my shame met no earthly match when I could not return to Chadwick later that week with his beloved Yuelfrik by my side...

I remember that day in grueling detail: the day that Yuelfrik envoided—took to the skies alongside the seasonal flight of the valkyries. He heaved himself up onto the wooden platform high up in the tree with his stiff arms, and he lay for a minute collecting himself and trying to retrieve his breath as usual. His voluptuous figure rippled mildly as his bones shivered with exhaustion. Something far off caught his eye, and he tip-toed to the ledge to get the best look. Excited and terrified, his facial expressions varied drastically, and he began to sign his message, beaming down his update. He would never finish dancing that message. He hopped on one foot, arms outstretched, revealing his true wingspan to best maintain his poor balance, as a part of a common movement that began a variety of our gestures.

But suddenly, as he bounced on his toes, a gust of wind caught him, and, suspended in mid-air, the wind swept him away.

101

The blubbery skin that drooped from his biceps acted as effective sails, and the powerful breeze carried him off through the clouds. His rubbery masts rippled as he entered the vortex of a land far away. Enveloped by the clouds and shrouded by mist, Yuelfrik simply vanished into the horizon.

I waited impatiently for Yuelfrik to float back into the hungry enclosure of my outstretched arms.

He never did.

Hours passed before I felt worthy enough of existence to move a muscle. Having finally buried enough of my shame to return to the bungalow, I stood on my uncle's porch disheveled, unsure, and a little dirty, but hopeful. Though the trifles of Yuelfrik's demise would roll from my conscience like raindrops, the concern of Uncle Chadwick's reprimanding hand lay heavy on my heart, just as it would soon lay heavy on my bum. I wouldn't mind the spanking, but his disappointment would be punishment enough. My uncle opened the door and peered out of the dark, sunken eye sockets that resided deep in his lined face.

"Eeh... It's Larwa, I suppose," he rasped, acknowledging me. He sucked a long whiff of fresh air through his thin, pointy nose, and his dry lips curled into a smile. Anyone could tell it was the first time he had taken the time away from his work to indulge himself in the luxurious pastime of inhaling in several years. He was repulsively malnourished, and he had aged drastically since I had last seen him—a mere six hours ago. He appeared to be a creature of about 700 years old at first sight, but then one realized that was highly irrational. He led me inside. I came bearing grim news and shifting awkwardly about, but my teeth broke the cooing silence with nervous chatter.

"Yuelfrik treads lightly upon the territories of moon men, and he whistles softly through the bombardment of stars. We can only reach for him now. He transforms into a sparkle of the night," I stuttered through closed teeth. I attempted to sugarcoat his death and soothe my uncle with serenading words. My monotone mumblings, however, came across as sardonic and careless.

My uncle would not expose his weeping self to me. "Go then, howl into the darkness and reach for the stars! Reach for my boy, and pick him from the night sky!" I felt a wind suck me from the residence, and the door similarly sucked closed. He regressed into the holds of the shadowy shed, not to exit for three winters.

15: PARADES OF EXORBITANCE IN THE PALACE

Three years passed with dreadful lethargy. My uncle remained in the shed like a scaly armadillo in a hole. As I passed him by, I heard the metronomic pounding of his iron thumper–the hammer that slammed the metal sheets and shaped them to the liking of his imagination. I trudged by his shed exiting our tawny brown house, built with only two walls, as I commuted to my laboring duties each day, and the familiar discordant clatter of metallic labor warmed my heart, for it alone ascertained that my uncle yet lived. The hollow echo rang in harmonic succession and flooded the vibrational palette of my ear drums.

Curiously, the thundering echoes died down to a creaking metal whisper–a softer tintinnabulation that rang more smoothly, but more ominously and somberly. Intrigued, I encroached upon the shed, transgressing on the secretive work of Uncle Chadwick, and entered.

I came to a work table on which lay a conglomeration of various tools, measuring devices, and building materials, and I saw him craned over a rusted contraption, a hunch in his back and a crick in his neck. His organs bulged through a constricting layer of leathery skin. I felt the sickle of the Grim Reaper tickle the nape of my neck as He inspected the room as well. A cold silence ensued as I groped my emotions for their linguistic song.

"Eat, please; give me one silver and I will fetch you bread!" I finally begged, my voice trembling with the terrible sadness that strangled my words. He did not acknowledge me for a few moments more. The sight of his carcass withering as the elements battered away at his dissolving body agonized me.

"Take yourself a breather dear Uncle! You slave away at this machine every day and forget to eat!"

"I have nothing; you will next fetch me in the smother. I've finished with my gliding contraption; all is spent," my uncle divulged to me. "And it is good that you came before the moon, because on this day, I will depart with the sun." The words came as a harder spank than any his hand could have delivered. It had clearly been my fault, I thought. His old heart was weak and fragile, and he reminded me nothing of his once-youthful self, the man who had so gracefully tended to me as a child and who had saved me from certain starvation. It had been the news of his son's disappearance that had triggered his heart failure.

"This is my fault. Isn't it?" He made eye contact without answering. "Isn't it?"

"I am tired, Larwa. I am tired," he finally responded with mild irritation. The more I considered it, the more sense it made. He had never loved me as he did Yuelfrik, and as his body continued to exponentially age, the agony of clinging to life became increasingly demanding; holding on would be pointless without his beloved Yuelfrik for whom to live. The science becomes simple when those irrational impulses of attachment are denied. Existence becomes unreasonable.

"I believe Yuelfrik may still linger in our atmosphere. Use this gliding machine and find my son roaming the clouds so I don't have to find him roaming the nether," he prayed to me, hand on my shoulder. Darkness blanketed the dead land in the hour of his death. There was nothing else to it; he simply released. It was all very clean and easy. I looked upon him for a moment, then diverted my gaze to the corpse's whimsical creation.

They were two crudely yet scientifically smithed wings, spanning over ten feet and scraping the floor loudly as the wearer walked. Now I could pursue Uncle's target on the trajectory Yuelfrik himself had taken: the almighty life-giving westerly winds, bringers of water and sustenance. I did believe Yuelfrik and his father reunited in the nether or perhaps the icy tundra of Niflheim, but I would despondently search for him in the clouds nonetheless.

I fastened the leather thongs of the wings to my shoulders and forearms. Then, I scaled an ancient pine until I could no longer see the ground; in fact, I could not see anything–not through the flight goggles that I ingeniously crafted from twigs and leaves. They provided comfort, warmth, and protection from the flotsam air particles and buzzing gnats. But, unfortunately, the goggles did not grant me vision of anything–a compromise I was willing to make. The tender twiglings clung tenaciously to the inside cusps of my ears as I proudly readied myself for the flight.

"Into oblivion!" I thundered into the open skies. I leapt gracefully and dove directly into the ground, shapeshifting into the form of a predator drone. Much to my dismay, the predator after which the drone whose form I took was modeled was a handicapped chihuahua. The heavy metal wings landed on top of me and detached my scapulas as my limbs clumsily rolled over each other and slapped against the dirt. The crunch of my skeletal intricacies resonated audibly to all dwellers of the forest, but not loudly enough to deter me. I initiated my second attempt by climbing the next tree over–a thinner pine with a less perilous stature. I pounced again and failed to catch a gust of wind. This time, my point of impact rested about another ten feet from my original starting point. I continued hopping from the branches to the roots of the next tree over for hours, never managing to fly for longer than a couple of seconds at a time, until I accidentally fell into a luxurious and well-fortified royal outpost adorned with numerous statues of Krüstof mingling with the gods. Isolated in this clearing shone the residency of the royals, miles from any charted villages. Was this Krustof's hidden Royal Palace—the one of legend?

I crept silently, my wings dragging a few feet behind on the cobblestone walkway. They scraped the rocks and sparked with each step, shooting metallic wails of agony into the uncaring forest. Although they were indeed fine pieces of equipment, I decided that lugging all that weight around was just unnecessary cardio and depleted my boyish stamina. Molting like a locust, I removed the immense metal frame and sagged it off my shoulders, and I left the obnoxious wings stowed in the cover of a bush. I slithered by a window and caught a glimpse of a goofy nobleman in the nude. I chuckled softly and jogged on.

Finally, I came to a grand palace surrounded by heated coy ponds and rich gardens. Guest wings stretched from the central hall, and fountains featuring granite carvings invited courtmen to stay as lifelike gargoyles perched upon spiraling towers of golden adornments, deterring any wandering peasants from entering the royal residency. Primitive growls and bellows pierced the still air, slicing the moonlit peace into a fragmented mess of sour dissonance. The rotting crab moltings scattered around the swimming pool told me that Krüstof's home stood before me.

107

I vaulted over the fence of the central palace and army-crawled around the corner, where I saw a side entrance to the building guarded by a well-built rifleman. Much to my advantage, a royal secretary and his feeble maiden strolled by, stopping me dead in my tracks. The noble frog couple halted in front of a puddle—which could easily have been avoided through a slight horizontal detour en route—and flared their nasal slits, signaling the guard to pay homage. He promptly dropped flat across the ground to provide cushioning, and the first-class amphibians poised and hobbled across his back. The pampered frog woman hooked her elbow round her mate as she stumbled across the uneven surface; the two appeared very off-balance on only two legs and with tiny leather clogs on—a queer and conveniently distracting sight indeed. I carefully snuck past the preoccupied guard and ventured inside.

I entered through the mud-room and stumbled upon a rather peculiar fascination. Down the hall, at the end of the footprints, past the coat hangers, there hunched a frail old man over a clay pot. Two microscope lenses extended from his eyes, and two beautifully decorated pots balanced on either side of the entrance. The vase sprouted beautiful grass, which had been pruned with an elegant finesse; each individual blade had been artfully snipped away into intricate designs of feathers or regal swirls. The man kept a toolbox by his side, complete with an extra pair of mini scissors and a mini magnifying glass to gaze through souls with microscope vision. The pot on the left was complete and ready for a welcome display; the second, however, would require several more winters before earning the right to boast completion. The artist had labored his entire life, dedicating his years to a lost craft. He had never felt the release of rest, and his white beard grew so long that the maids had come by and knitted the facial hair into a doormat. Lost in the intensity of his focus, the old artist did not notice me wipe my feet on his beard or hear me stub my toe on the annoyingly positioned door as I clammered into the next hall in a fit of whispered curses.

As I entered, the sultry moisture that plagued the denture-hall instantly overcame my pores. Denchers of the nobility lay organized in a shelf by saliva gleam order, and aristocrats removed them when entering a host's house as a sign that they were comfortable (the clasps of the gum spikes lining the adhesion ridge caused immense oral throbbing and distress to the wearer). Nature viewing optical apparati, commonly called "nature specs," hung from racks mounted on the wall. In order to take in more nature from the gardens, the bourgeois sported thin, iron, spectacle-like clamps that they tightened until their eyes bulged out of their sockets and their veins nearly burst. The mucus membranes swelled until they produced enough iris fluid to drip profusely, but increased bloodflow to the eye degraded their corneas to irritated sacs of blood and lens mucus. This is, in fact, obsolete because the near-three-hundred-sixty-degree visibility was well worth the retinal overhand that bounced violently with every step. I waded through the lung-filling clouds of the hookah-puffing frogs and observed them waft one another's canisters of crimp cut tobacco. They focused hard not to blush while they flattered each other with charming remarks that commended the fine intricacies of the red man's leaf. In a breath I slipped under the velvet curtain that partitioned the frogs from the mammals of the opium lounge. Inhaling the soothing fragrance, I embodied the mass of the euphoric smoke and mingled my way

109

through the conglomeration of strange furry creatures, occasionally floating into their lungs and sailing out in the next breath. Offended by the overwhelming buzz of the puncturing vapors, I passed them by and came to a maintenance entrance of the kitchen.

Several chefs ordered their bustling sous chefs about the cacophonous stoves and refrigerators, while well-groomed waiters briskly strode in to retrieve fresh platters stacked high with nutmeg-infused toucan tongue and pickled-in fungal rots atop a firm bed of bitter sharkfin risotto. They hastily doled out flying spoonfuls of congealed tofu gravy, curdled sour cream flatbreads, wood pulp, and caviar squeezed straight from a land salmon's womb, doused in a light buttermilk vinaigrette.

I pressed down hard on the ridge of my temples and shrunk to the size of a toy lunker. Why I shrank after massaging my temples I never understood, but I began to quake and assumed that I would soon enlarge to regular size, so I wasted no time, immediately inspecting the scene in closer quarters than would have been possible without shrinkage. As I whistled through the air like a wafering dragonfly banished from his master's keep, I was unforeseen. I dove into a bowl of steaming soup being delivered to the Duke of Pinkus. The nonchalant Duke made casual conversation with dinner mates as he dipped his spoon into the bowl. The spoon made acquaintance with me immediately, but it dismissed itself soon after. A sudden guilt plagued my conscious, and I felt that my connaissance of the soup arose as a direct result of cheating. I pardoned my transgression, but it was sinisterly sly to utilize such an unfair tactic; from that day forward, I would shrink no more.

I emerged from the soup and slithered up a light fixture, hoisting my way up a lamp in the corner as my body eased into its prior form. With dexterous hands, I skillfully gripped the golden stem of the lamp and maneuvered to the peak like a gecko. My body, crammed betwixt the shallow crevice encompassed by the paisley lamp-shade, shifted about feverishly, for the thin fibers of the lamp-shade chafed my hammies. I squatted atop the bulb, and I malignantly cast my sprawling shadow upon the ceiling; it watched them, practically tickling the tops of the guests' heads. It devoured them in darkness, saving the greedy from themselves. The silhouette that danced upon the ceiling was fortunately ignored by the party-goers, and, yet again, unforeseen.

The only familiar face present belonged to a lizard aficionado, appropriately dubbed The Reptilian. I had often glimpsed the crocodilian connoisseur on his way to enter his steamy, dank underground laboratory. Krüstof had hired him along with a young, promising officer by the name of Yægelshmick, who he hoped would one day take the Reptilian's place after the aging officer's health deteriorated, as royal advisors and scientific researchers. The skink-savvy dilettante's title was accurate, for his home took the shape of a smoothly rounded, greenhouse-like dome, and his floors were coated by desert-red sand, imported from the fanciest Persian vendors. Within the perimeter of the glass dome, his scaly beasts did roam free. Rumor had it that his snakes were sentenced with snuggling and his lizards condemned to constant cuddling, and though he loved his cold blooded companions, he could never aspire to attain their lifestyle. His appearance was disappointingly human; his white skin glowed with pallor, and his inability to stick to walls and surfaces as he walked discouraged him greatly. One could easily identify the glowing envy in his eyes as he constantly stroked the lizards that dangled from his vest and basked on the overhangs of his breast plate. His hat was an eloquent conglomerate of reptile skins taken from hundreds of different species, coupled with his amber-preserved crocodilian-eyeball-encrusted, bronze scarf. As he often bragged, this masterpiece alone was worth as much as the entire sector, and it was still the least expensive of all his clothing items. His suit was forged from melted lizard skeletons, decorated with strips of alligator leather and rings of fossilized tasmanian devil teeth. His comportment managed to distance him from the face-stuffed babbling and dewlap warbling contendants, and he took rather to his sciences than appeasing a trifling chatter with an even more insincere comment. The noise all mixed and hummed to him like a perturbing bee, and he put it to the back of his mind and cleared space to theorize. A recluse of strange and fancy, he collected my interest longer than did most of the other comparatively commonplace guests.

Then, another detached ornament of the crowd caught my drifting glance and managed to hold it as I inspected him. This dapperly dressed wiry beaked man sat away from any table, isolated yet dignified in his satisfied solitude. Tall and thin, he did his expertly-tailored outfit justice. He sat slender and elegant, exercising impeccable posture. He planted his entitled tailfeathers firmly into the cushioned stool, which slightly enveloped his bony rump, but he remained stiff and steady as a sunflower, ever erect during summer's lease. He sank into his pillowed perch with an awkwardly charming finesse, distinguished in his regal high-stool. His copious pins, medallions, and an honorary sash draped over his broad shoulders and climbed across his proud chest like gleaming water droplets running down vines on a long-revered cherry blossom tree. Established as stump-thick roots he was in prestige, yet even in perfect stillness, he fully captured the essence of suave navigation, so thoroughly decorated with streaming ribbons and flowing silks. A bowling hat badged by a sparkling emblem teetered atop his wrinkly and sparsely-feathered scalp. It was an honor to the hat–being on his head. His lanky legs crossed above the knee, raising his droll footwear to the attention of those walking by. He wagged his foot gently, boasting a majestically forged buckle and a lustrous diamond perched on the tip of the toe curl of his enchanting shoes. The alligator leather's luminous shine delivered a soft cloud of brass glow to the ground he graced with his glorious presence. Gaudy, perhaps, but he was undeniably superior to all. Above the rest, his magnificent beak protruded several inches from his prominent jaw like an outstretched hand demanding universal respect. The aggressively intellectual posturing, paired with his interesting loafers, was a bold move. However, the passers-by were too busy racing one another to the buffets, chewed food still dripping from their flapping lips, to pay the birdman's boasts any mind.

A party of offensively loquacious noblemen and their wives chortled away at the table nearest to the bird man. One of the wives laughed a little too loudly at a distasteful jest. Consequently, the ornithological legend averted his dreamy gaze from his platter to redirect it to the alpha male of the group and unfortunately administered him the most intense staredown ever experienced by a

113

piteous mortal. His victim was first paralyzed in seizure-inducing eye contact, and the man felt himself jerk his head away and down at his plate as if he had been cross-faced by a rambunctious phantom. The birdman's beady black eyes raged silently like a quiet ocean storm in the starkest darkness of night; all ships would be tossed. The feathery noble suddenly threw his head back and his shoulders forward with a bitterly sardonic cackle, and the high-pitched and mocking guffaw cut the ambiance of the dining hall so cleanly that plenty of room remained for its soaking plus one: its ruthless sarcasm. Soft echoes of the grating squawk dissolved into the deafening silence, bouncing the caw across the walls and recycling its annoyance. This putrid aroma of a rotten nut moistened by sprites suddenly seeped from the crevice of submissionary humiliation and explored the nasal cavities of the terrified victims, daring them to challenge the authority of the birdman. It sounded as though the oblivious and overly zealful birdman had attempted to take part in the playful banter, but his crude, phony chirp was all too brash. The silence was less awkward or sorrowful but painful, and the flushed dinner attendants cringed and gnashed their teeth. They quickly took to even more pitiful excuses to escape and deliver themselves from the aching humiliation that lingered in the room and stabbed at everyone like a drunk homeless man.

"I think I need to take you to the hospital!" urgently muttered one of the men to his meaty wife as he rapidly stuffed his pockets with leftovers.

"Yes." she hurriedly replied with wide eyes full of fear. "I think I've broken my arms!" she exclaimed. Tabular evacuation proceeded in mere seconds, and the birdman looked back to whatever had held his gaze before. He slowly curled his spindly fingers over his knee once more, causing his many military and sporting rings to glint in the chandelier light. He had parted a crowd; they were furious, yes. They had not known that they were being eavesdropped upon, and along with this violation, they felt embarrassed about the trivial nature of their discussion. Simple matters such as subordinate gossips and personal ramblings were a disgrace in the eyes of such a decorated gentleman. I felt the warmth of my rosey cheeks; I practically glowed with embarrassment along with the scuttling guests. The awkward vibe that was left hanging in the air long after the room emptied drove me off as well. Anyhow, nothing remained from which to derive entertainment.

I strolled down the deserted corridor. Where exactly the royal attendants did take refuge from the savage vocal contractions of the feathery fiend, I did not know or care. The question would not plague me, but perhaps, I contemplated, they would recollect themselves in their respective rooms of the sleeping chambers in the left wing of the palace. I knew I would not be seen here, for surely only the birdman's soul dwelled in the right wing of the palace with me. Perched and immovable, he breathed elegantly, still sitting upon his stool that I had imagined. Even his lungs showed style, for he inhaled in a sort of rhythmic pattern—one that encouraged onlookers to tap their feet in step with his musical organs. But I digress.

Pottery and ceramic beauties lined the halls, ceilings painted to match the heavens. As I continued through the decorous hallways, gilded generously with sapphire and emerald, I approached a grand door and barrel-rolled the remaining stretch of the hall over to it like a true spy man. I breached the door with a stern front kick and executed another roll. The wood shattered silently. I had trespassed upon Krüstof's holding.

Krüstof peered over the head of his recliner, but he did not see me prostrate upon the floor. I stood behind him and stuck my finger in his ear as I walked past. He looked about fervently, and his dewlap wagged as he blubbered like a spook and returned to his reading*. A dastardly prank, and a childish one at that. I continued on into his sleeping quarters and poured his contact solution into the sink. I drew him a bath but allowed the water to pour over the brim and to further splatter the floor. Then I whirled around with a devious grin plastered on my face. I opened his nightstand and withdrew a bag labeled "Krüstof's Finest Sparkling Maggots." I emptied the casing and pounded them on the nightstand until they sloshed and squirted at every jab in a thick goo; then I submerged my hands in it and crushed the survivors. Weird, one might think, but I had vaguely formed a plan.

*As a young child the abstract concepts of human-self-consumption enthralled me. I am sure the rat children with which I associated myself in my youth were influenced by my amateur teachings and most likely took a droll liking to my radical preaching. As the sands of time inevitably continued to wash over memories, they were lost, only to be rediscovered, surfacing in my research during my adolescence. Realizing that autocannibalism was solely categorized into vague and widely inaccurate subsections, there dwelled *a force beckoning within me to share my concepts and research with other scholars. Autosacrophagy (or autocannibalism) should not be linked to psychological manipulation, forced punishment, or a symptom of a disorder, but rather regarded as a natural occurrence in the absence of conscience or even further to be broadly accepted as a deliberate choice. Self-consumption is the instinctive and logical path through which such a deranged individual must travel, seen to that individual as only another ordinary truth. In the passive mind, when the world is processed in waves of realization but drifts relatively near the brink of complete [?] Accidental consumption is not [LOST IN TRANSLATION].*

Case Study:

Former pizza delivery specialist and Japanese social phenomenon Yuta Nabungo is currently the only known human being to fully consume his own body. Although not overweight or even hefty in any sense, Nabungo supplemented his pizza income with a lesser-known form of professional eating that required him to consume obscene amounts of food for the pleasure of an audience. He worked a number of years, late in his life, as a Japanese Messy Boy in the upper class Yamanote quarter of Tokyo, entertaining lonely, middle-aged Japanese trophy wives neglected by their husbands who had grown tired of their female companions. These women paid Nabungo handsomely for the opportunity to watch him devour heaping plates of sticky wet foods, such as barbecue ribs or spaghetti, with his bare hands. Nabungo would don only a bib and diaper in attempt to get his entire body as messy as possible. In the 2004 Kabukicho Morality Exhibition, Yuta immortalized his family name by managing to completely eat himself, a feat beforehand thought by scientific authorities to be entirely impossible and ridiculous. Shocking the world, Yuta fastened his messy boy bib and chowed down until he was gone, disproving the old outdated belief system in only 15:04. The prospect of consuming 146 lbs. (Nabungo's weight at his most recent doctor's visit prior to his death) of raw meat and bone is unthinkable to any human, especially when that crude cuisine once constituted one's own actual body. Yet to the mighty little champion Nabungo, this prospect in fact was thinkable and even achievable. This unexpected outcome was made possible by Nabungo's preemptive genius. A Kabukichoi Morality Exhibition employee, Yasamuta Oise, recounts her interaction with Nabungo on the day of his noble feat. She claims to have asked him how he could possibly eat such a "large portion" of his own body after he finished his right leg. The 23-year-old legend allegedly explained that he had not eaten anything all day in preparation for the event. Nabungo went about the formidable task in what is now known as the most efficient and logical way to eat oneself: first, Nabungo ate all of his hair to prevent unnecessary early bleeding. The next step carried capital cruciality: Nabungo severed a thin strip of his upper body, stretching from his shoulder blades to underarms. This enabled Yuta to eat his own lower body without experiencing any pain, at least in a physical sense. Eating oneself was considered shameful in the Tokyo slum that invested so heavily in defending one's honor and putting up a hard front at all times. Finishing oneself entirely, however, remains a commendable act that demands the respect of all life in the universe. The stadium shook with the roars of jeering spectators, who were throwing broken beer bottles and spitting at Yuta. Our righteous hero paid no mind, steadily devouring himself bottom to top, toes to nipples. Fortunately, Yuta's disembowelment prevented him from feeling or actually being full, for whatever he masticated simply squirted out of his lower esophagus, which connected to no stomach. After eating the disconnected portion, Yuta moved on to the delicacy of his hands and arms. Yuta supposedly showed great pain in biting through these sensitive nerve endings, but he did not falter for the slightest moment. By this point, the meth heads and designer jean-clad Yakuza gangsters in the stands were rioting in support of Yuta, placing bets and shooting each other. When finished with his arms and shoulders, Yuta hyperextended his mandible until his jaw had completed a full 360 degree chomp, encircling his skull, and therefore

finishing off his entire body, leaving behind a
steaming pile of carnal pulp, a feast for the flies,
and a grease-stained pizza delivery hat,
notoriously worn backwards. Japanese SWAT
forces were obligated to use lethal force to
suppress the insane violence that followed
Nabungo's fabled success.

Yuta's bedroom in his parents' home has
since been converted into a shrine to his
gourmandizationary excellence where inspired film
producers and confused college students may
now visit for a modest price. The exhibit includes
an empty pizza box and a poster of a hefty
American woman straddling the hood of a vintage
Ford Mustang. Yuta has been described by his
friends as "chill" and "mild-mannered." Yuta's
mother admits that she is extremely proud of her
son, but complains the fame and family glory can
never fill the void in an ex-mother's heart. (Due to
an astonishingly high concentration of
amphetamine addicts drawn by the opportunity to
sell shabu to the gangbangers and weirdos that
attended the event, the annual games never
returned after 2005, inscribing Nabungo's already
untouchable record in stone.)*

I smeared the white paste all over my face and shaved my
head with Krüstof's razor, leaving the hair to itch him in his bed. I
stole his sheets and wrapped myself loosely, practicing my
roundhouse on Krüstof's bedside lamp, after which my foot got
stuck in the wall. Krüstof waddled in soon after and gasped; I could

tell he felt emotionally betrayed, but I didn't care. I chucked his nighttime easy reading into his forehead, tore my ankle from the wall, and bounded out of the palace, the white maggogoo dripping from my moist cheek. Distraught, his primordial instinct commanded him to feign death at the sight of me, who he thought was a haunting specter. He rocked on his back like a dead roach as I pressed through the halls of the palace, wooing like a ghost.

I whizzed around on the steam of a fart, and I thought I might pass by the dining hall, which had previously been cleared by the birdman, to snag a taste of the extraterrestrial poultry about which the royals could not stop jabbering. I hovered in the doorway and observed that a small group of nobleman had amassed again in front of a magician. Distracted by fear of the return of the birdman, who would certainly make the social situation embarrassing and awkward, the noblemen did not notice the mediocrity of the magician's card tricks.

The magician asked an anxious onlooker to choose a card, and the man did so absentmindedly, never making eye contact with the wizard and instead shifting his gaze nervously about the corridor, his teeth clattering and his abdomen tight with apprehension. The magician snatched the card from the man's limp fingers, whipped a crimson permanent marker out from his coat, drew a sloppy circle on the card, and returned it to its chooser.

"You have CIRCLE!" the wizard proudly exclaimed, an optimistic smile creeping along his wrinkled jowls. The nobleman, distraught, glanced momentarily at the card and offered a singular clap in return, never ocularly acknowledging the magician and never focusing his stare upon any one object for more than a half-second.

121

Dreledon the Dinklehead

In his delight at the man's approval, the magician twirled about his toes and hummed a dainty tune, twiddling his fingers and chuckling satisfactorily. His custom-made name tag slipped off his robe and breezed over to my foot, glistening in black lettering. On it breathed a stupid name: "Dreledon." Taking advantage of the distracted nobility, I decided to make my leave. I headbutted the doorway and defecated on my way out the Chancellor's palace.

16: Children of the Same Crop

Later that day, I skipped gaily to Uncle Chadwick's home. His festering corpse rotted, and flies thrived on his flesh, laying their eggs and spawning maggots exponentially; the parabola of maggotial population displayed clearly in my mind, graphed with exact measurements along both the x and y axes. Fly spawn filled his bones in place of long-decayed marrow and held his skeletal structure loosely. I reached my hand into his bloody neck and rummaged my way through his swollen throat, finding exit through his sinewy jaw and stabbing my fingers securely into his richly infected gums, whose flexible surface swallowed my fingernails so that I could malleably control his mouth and lips by puppeteering and twisting my digits. At first, it was a complex and nearly impossible task, but I was deranged and desperate. I had lost my Uncle—the last adult I trusted—and the last home I could hope for. I was young and blinded by grief, and in my denial I decided to attempt to animate him into life once more. After hours of practice, my artificial movement of his supple lips seemed even more lifelike than his own, and I even convinced myself that he was alive, forgetting entirely that my hand inside his esophagus moved his jaw and that my voice mimicked his. I gave Uncle Chadwick's corpse its first words.

"Larwa! My sweet!" I said through my uncle's mouth. "How is my favorite son?" My uncle had never called me "son" before, and the words warmed my heart immensely, especially that it was I, not Yuelfrik, who was his favorite this time.

"Just fine!" I replied. But I then remembered my sin: I had set out to find Yuelfrik but returned empty handed. I had failed, and once my uncle heard this, he would surely reconsider his favoritism. I became immensely nervous, and sweat poured profusely from my brow. Grimacing, I feared my uncle's dreaded hand would soon meet my backside. I looked at it, and in death it seemed doubly menacing, maggots crawling to and fro and swallowing what skin had yet to decay. "Um, that's it! NO MORE QUESTIONS NOW! I HAVE NOTHING LEFT TO SAY NOW!" I screamed in terror. I released his jaw and sprinted from the room.

After a few minutes of fear, I gathered my courage and stepped back into my uncle's room. He looked expectantly at my worried eyes, but my confidence stayed true, and I slipped my hand back into his throat.

"What's that on your face?" my uncle inquired.

"Oh, this?" I replied, referring to the maggot-white coloring on my cheeks. "I smeared some maggots on there..." I worried he would further query where I obtained the maggots, revealing that I hadn't looked diligently for my cousin but had instead been dilly dallying, but his mind had clearly been provoked to reveal to me a local legend.

"Your skin is as white as that of the Ghost Boy!" He excitedly claimed. "How I used to love that tale! All the villagers know it, you know. The respectable ones, at least. Do you?"

"Um... I don't think many people know about that," I nervously retorted, worried that my uncle might think I wasn't cool enough to know about this so-called Ghost Boy.

"Yes, everyone does! Goodness, I must tell you! Why, what would you do if your boss talked about it at work? Why, you wouldn't be able to chime in with helpful input!" He reasoned. "Well, here goes."

"He is known by many names and has multiple variations, though it is unanimously agreed that the boy's naught but an unearthly spectre from another dimension, and he is known simply as the Ghost Boy, for he eluded the grasp of chastisement in the way only an intangible spirit could. Legend has it that he killed the previous Chancellor of Punishment, Olaf, and proceeded to slaughter millions of maggots before they quenched his rebellious thirst," Uncle Chadwick recounted. I listened intently as he recited a handful of tales that characterized this prolific figure: how he defeated the peg-legged octopus in the forest; how he bested Lord Cornwalch in a game of fruitsmoop; how he crafted a hauling contraption to carry the incredibly obese Norwegian Whaleman from the plains on which he had inexplicably manifested to the ocean. Yes, various seemingly impossible deeds decorated this Ghost Boy's resumé, but he was characterized most often by one especially significant feat: he had gone against the divine will of the Chancellor, and, as they told, after killing him, led his own rebellious spirit to the grave in the most honorable of manners. My uncle recounted the myth to my anxiously anticipating ears:

"This Ghost Boy was a fighter. He swung his fists and slung swift kicks amidst his ghastly mist. He ran till his rubber burned and melted his legs into a crumpled heap. His gelatinous ghost loins dripped to the cold, unforgiving floor. The resounding smack of the phantom jelly filled the moist cellar like an inflamed toad bouncing his lumpily swollen amphibious body. He decreased in stature as his legs melted, but gained much fake fat. The translucent chunkiness glimmered in the faint light of the bioluminescent maggot experiment, and the vat creaked and churned as the severely deformed test subjects wailed in agony. The glowing burned their tukuses; it seared their fleshy maggot shit. The Ghost Boy's personal mass drooped to the cinder block floor and took shape of a scraggly lark egg. His face floated down the ectoplasm waterfall like an unframed portrait cast from Sputnik II into the gentle caress of the cosmic westerlies. His befuddled expression lay atop his jiggly chest, and his limbs withdrew into his newfound specto-mollusk body like a frightened turtle. All of his gains: lost. All of his pain: wasted. The enraged slug lad shimmied to the incubatory maggot vats and stretched himself out a thick, slimy neck. He repeatedly slammed his face into the plexiglass until the thorny, fibrous shards lined the sweaty folds of his hearty chops. He permitted himself one strident vengeance howl.

'"YÆAAAAAAHHHHSSSS!' he squealed. The raspy victory shriek shook the testicular fortitude of every individual frankenmaggot, for the malicious ghost slug was upon them. He continued face-smashing the helpless feti into a gleimous maggot aioli. The lardy, halatinous, sinapistic paste crackled and festered. 'MYÆEEHH!' he gurgled. 'MAHATMA... MAGGOT... COOL!' he chanted vigorously. The maggots took his life."

Until that moment I had never considered that the almighty Krüstof or his maggots could be defeated. My childhood had persisted, plagued with tragic mortalities and unmatched grief. However, despite the horrid life I and most other villagers led, I now held a seed of hope to overthrow the oppressive government. If village people told tales of a wee boy who rebelled with otherworldly strength against the Soviets with unprecedented success, and they believed these tales avidly, then perhaps the people could be rallied into believing another rebellious spirit... But my uncle's quavering voice interrupted this thought.

"What of Yuelfrik, then? Did you find him? Did the contraption work?" he wondered with obvious suspicion. Scraping my maggopasted visage into a jar, I returned to reality, and my anxiety returned with me.

"Uhh, I have to go potty! BYE!" I stammered as I stumbled away once more, wiping my uncle's neck blood off my dampened hand. It had become evident that my uncle would soon conclude that I had not found Yuelfrik as long as I continued to converse so frequently with him. But I enjoyed his tales, no matter how fictional and incoherrent I found them, and I yearned to hear more. It was clear that I had to find Yuelfrik, or, since this seemed impossible given the vastness of the land he might occupy, create a Yuelfrik of my own. After stowing the jar in my medicine cabinet, I went to work.

I stuffed straw into some of my old, unfitting rags. I used my own globby spit to hold together the insides, for it was so dry that it absorbed the air's nearby moisture and expanded into a sort of solid sponge, easily consolidating straws within each bubble. I created two blobs of straw: one small circle to serve as his cranium, and a second ovular shape to encompass his torso. On the front of the rags, I wrote sloppily in ink: "I AM YUELFRIK." Two ink dots splattered on the ball that was his head, accompanied by a wavering smile. I added a hat, shoes, and thick sticks, creating a very messily constituted version of my lost cousin. It stood about two feet tall and barely resembled a human, but, I considered, my uncle wouldn't notice. After all, he had been dead for some time, and his eyes weren't quite what they used to be.

"Good news!" I announced, beaming as I entered the room flaunting my makeshift cousin. "I found Yuelfrik!"

"Oh, my!" He exclaimed. "My beautiful Yuelfrik!" His eyes filled with dry tears, but as they rolled down his cheek they slipped through the cracks of his exposed muscle. "I was beginning to think you hadn't found him," he stated, a hint of reprimand in his now stern voice.

My nerves returned, and my bowels clenched. "No, uncle! Of course I found him! Why, he's right here." I reminded my critical uncle that Yuelfrik was here, in my hand, and his tension seemed to ease. He was convinced, I thought. The plan proved a total success, and I could now freely ask him to tell me another story—one of the few sources of entertainment that existed in this bleak society.

"Uncle Chadwick, can you tell me a story now!?" I demanded, indignantly believing that my minimal effort to convince him of Yuelfrik's persisting existence merited the reward of an intriguing tale.

"Of course, son," he replied, the excitement he had felt before now dimmed by his slight doubt in Yuelfrik's reality.

"This is not a lie," Uncle Chadwick began. "Upon the transatlantic capture, all Polish infidels were banished to this forgotten land of Grunty Kraba, former home of the ancient Zad capitalist barbarians. Their victorious conquest provided the Soviets

129

a much needed sanctuary for nefarious enterprises, such as quartering their Slavic subjects. Shipped by barrel, one by one, the political refugees crashed ashore, thoroughly pickled by the salty sea air. Contrary to popular belief, those who emerged from the barnacled barrels were not the same who went in, for their confinements took decades to see the bliss of land after their departure from Russia. Within their walls, therefore, lived not only one person, but an entire lineage. Indeed, as many as a dozen generations of a single family endured crampedly within each barrel, and a handful of these generations lived and died having never seen the luxury of dry terrain. Their bones contorted into horrible arrangements so that they could all fit inside their tiny homes, and the ecosystem within descended into cannibalism due to the lack of another stable food source. The resulting species went to pot, becoming one of malnourished weakness and deranged savagery, so that the entirety of the exported Polish people evolved into a sub-human object of hatred, alienated by the Russians as a failed transport and no longer considered their biological equals."

Fact: this is the worst thing that has ever happened to the Polish people.

EXCLUSIVE BONUS FACTOID: Australia is the only country to also be considered a continent.

"Of course, not all the barrels shipped directly into the Americas, for the Soviets, like all respectable citizens of Earth, knew that there existed no direct sea route from Russia into the north American territories; the map simply does not connect the two Pacific Oceans. Thus, naturally, all barrels were rolled down to the Iberian Peninsula and then shipped from Spain, bound together loosely with rope, equipped with GPS in the form of a scholarly guideman in order to ascertain arrival at their destinations. It was also known that Chort, the barnacle-encrusted ghoul that pirated the Atlantic, would swallow any barrels that he crossed, having no mercy for those who intruded upon the waters he claimed as his, and so the barrels were to be shipped east through the Strait of Gibraltar, clockwise around the Horn of Africa, and west around South America, then climbing up the American western coast.

"Naturally, the Egyptians took tolls when foreigners crossed their seas, but the Russians, infamous for their stinginess, refused to pay monetarily. Instead, not willing to spur conflict, they made payment through a tax on their barrels of the exiled Polish peoples; one in every ten would be confiscated by the toll-takers. So it was; a substantial number of the outcasts, expecting to lay eyes upon the promised land they could freely call home, instead faced the desolate mistreatment of the warlords who purchased them from corrupt officials willing to accept bribery. Their fate remains to this day in the hands of the Egyptian lords who claimed them, but those who arrived in the Americas–the destination desired by their ancestors–would soon learn that their own destiny would be no sweeter. Of the Polish taxed into Africa and distributed by the Egyptian slave lords, we know not the rest of their story, but that of our own western ancestors is well-recorded and easily recountable.

"The Russian transport fleet untethered the barrels and allowed them to drift ashore. Now the human-cargo-filled barrels rolled onto the sandy beaches, spit out by the disgusted Ocean Man, who did not have a pallette for filthy, village-dwelling land-lubbers. The Polish emerged, jaded and disoriented by confusing

131

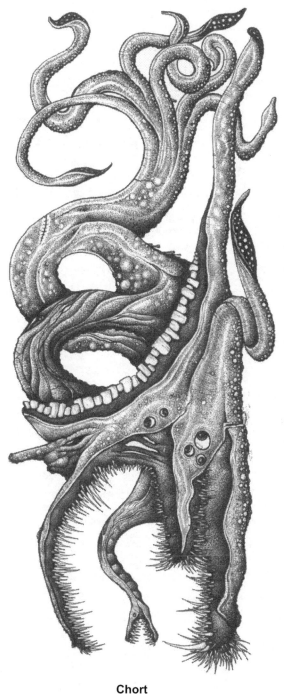

Chort

rays of the sweltering sun. Their skin clammed gruelingly, sleek and supple like high-quality lard, yet, paradoxically, as cracked as the sealed mouth of a mute skeletal warrior whose initial moisture had given way to dry parchedness lifetimes ago. Scrapes and rashes obliterated their inner thighs, making the task of walking one of excruciating pain. They stumbled on their swollen feet and fell, naked and sticky, into the sharp sand that encrusted their skin, shredding it raw with every shuffle so that their chafed bones only briefly bore the shelter of flesh. On the shore upon which they treaded gurgled the corpse of a bubbling beast, beached by the unforgiving current and coated in thick, grimy sea foam. Heavy char from the blistering sun embroidered its vulnerable skin, and its swollen, bloated belly churned and spumed with boiling gases. It lay, confecting and expanding with post-mortem digestive gusto, and seething steamily. The sloven atrocity bellowed in death, spewing molten acids and hot juice as its gaseous insides groaned like the weeping, the moaning, the vociferous gnashing of stained teeth resonating from the harbors of hell–teeth as physically stained as the psychologically tainted souls to which they were reluctantly attached. Distinct wrinkled segments comprised the beach-thing, a lengthy conglomerate of tanned pink flesh forming what could only be described as a gargantuan worm, far fatter in width than in length or height, but relatively smooth despite its gnarled growths, knobby and nautical as a cancerous willow. Scarred by the scorching heat and internally deteriorated at the hands of parasitic invaders, the swollen balloon-worm threatened to burst as internal gas pressure neared maximum capacity.

133

"Arriving closely behind: the fleet of deluxe wooden Russian vessels that shepherded the crude barrels. On these grand ships, matching the elegance of the Spanish Armada and its naval fleet at its peak, royal pilgrims tailed the bobbing barrels, anchoring and readying their skiffs. Intrigued by the legendary essence of the beached worm, noble men fumbled about and clamored into regal row-boats, gliding across the bay and then circling the worm. They inspected its bubbling stomach, which swelled disruptively as gases rumbled unventilated within their container and emitted several internally discomforted farts. The men scavenged for poking sticks with which to prod their discovery, remaining prudent not to tarnish their beautiful swords or bejeweled daggers. As soon as they decided that the meaty entity was safe for manhandling, they began slapping the latex skin fervently. A few men made a game of their finding, and they competed eagerly to find which sword's tip could plunge deepest into the Wormthing. However, their exaltation of wormy festivities was short-lived, for one gruff bellow echoed prominently from the intestines, and the surrounding men knew the capsule yearned to burst. They leapt from the blast radius and attempted to shield themselves behind beach shrubs or small mounds of sand that could barely rival a toddler's sandcastle, but their reflexes lacked the swiftness necessary to avoid a chunky glaze of pudgy grime. When their senses recollected, the revulsion from the explosion's epicenter proved unfathomably harrowing..." Uncle Chadwick paused to die a little more.

"Four hundred nude infant worms mewed and puked curdled blood as their shiny bottoms wallowed in the worm's decaying filth. The children gazed hungrily upon their discoverers, for their teething gums had yet to taste the luxury of fresh meat. Their bodies were strangely human, as if forged haphazardly by feral beings rather than an omniscient deity. The worm children were black, slender, and slimy, and their ebony blood pulsed clearly like ink through their gelatinous skin. When admiring the way their soft heads shined, one would wonder if they were rich as a bitch. The figures were haunting; an obsidian dust cloud seemed to linger upon them like death upon the gallows, and no appendages would dare cling to such physically atrocious beings from fear of loss of social reputation. Their bodies, unnaturally lanky and astoundingly muscular for such fetal pups, were composed of serpentine coils of grub-chub awkwardly conjoined to faces grotesquely resembling dismembered humans. Indeed, any human spotted sporting so embarrassing a visage would be instantly shamed by the beautiful masses; their jaws, from which sloppy gums and several rows of long spindling teeth protruded, were unhinged; their eyes were hollow with stark darkness, absorbing any light waves bold enough to attempt to impress their electromagnetic peers by approaching the aphotic entities. Their vascular system often webbed shut, congesting blood flow in gummy pools of warm body-syrups, and their eyelids similarly fused together after an extensive development period. As if such stiff biological anchorage did not suffice, their cruel creator granted them stagnant, congealed features and immobile rotting tongues, injecting the venom of severe and perpetual claustrophobia into their young minds, psychologically plaguing them for the rest of their short, agonius lives.

"As they slithered forward upon the onslaught, their long, delicate spines contorted violently, and the resulting sounds (i.e.

135

SPLACK; WHIQ; KRATZ) pierced the explorers' eardrums like a barrage of spear stabs. The men threw their hands over their pink ears, crest to lobe, and slung their heads around aimlessly, trying to escape the forsaken jurisdiction of this skeletal necrophonence, but the worm children slithered by the distraught masses and into the forests beyond the beach. The remaining men's much traumatized souls would linger on Grunty Kraba forever perturbed by the despair of uncertainty...

"And that, my son, is the legend of the worm children that reside on our Isle. Be it truth, I know not, but I do know this: if you should grow out of your innocence, persisting visions of the worm children will follow, like they follow all else on these lands," Uncle concluded.

Perhaps, I considered, the fear plaguing the populace enabled its toleration of Krüstof's iron fist. Perhaps it merely craved the Chancellor's unequivocal order. And suddenly I thought of how I might have been a wormchild, driven to recluse as my social peers disagreed with my ideas of hatred towards the government. I wondered, too, if Krüstof was a wormchild—if his youth'd been perturbed by exclusion...

17: FULLY TORQUED

The following was not inscribed in a rock:

"Krüstof! Don't play with the maggots now! They'll nibble on your fingertips!" cried Krüstof's meddling mother. How he abhorred that dreadful woman—her plumpish rolls mushing as she moistly trudged towards him to thwart his tomfoolery. He fondly observed her with his youthful eyes, disappointed in his rebellious loving attachment to his sweaty, maternal nemesis—one of the last personal mothers before the colony's singular breeder replaced them. She perspired soggily, her damp skin reminding him of his maggot companions. Oh, how he enjoyed those maggots of his! He tossed them in the air like a salad of acidic grime, and their greasy epidermal warts transferred seamlessly unto his calloused palm. They masticated his nails, bloodily gnawing his nerves into useless clotty blisters. He strangely loved the pungent ammonia smog the maggots ashamedly emitted, and he stuffed them into his nose, one by one, until his brain was filled with a happily thriving colony. His mouth followed suit; the nougat tartness of his nymphal companions titillated his taste-buds. He whipped them tearfully, and their lack of exoskeletal authority facilitated their combustion. His remorse was exquisitely spiritual, orgasmically stimulating his infantile psyche. CUR-THUNK—his mother swatted at his nape with the disciplinary force only a father could wield! This is the grand conundrum: a transgender, perhaps?

> Anonymous 1: "Conundrum? Hardly a perplexion really, wouldn't a quick 'check under the hood' suffice? Aha?"
> Anonymous 2: "As if! You just can't trust mechanics these days!"

He loved those larvomorphs more than anything, and the boys in his school teased him mercilessly for it. "Maggot-boy! Maggot-boy!" they scoffed. But today, he would not be stopped by his lactic ogre of a mother. Today her reign of milky oppression reached its finite conclusion. He swallowed handfuls of maggots, instantly granulating his esophagus as their sandy jaws frantically chewed his throat in desperation for escape. His mother loped by, unaware of his larval constitution, and Krüstof spat out clumps of the compressed maggot slime upon her dank bosom. They moved at millions of miles an hour, bending time fluently and shredding her skin into porridge. It melted steamily, radiating heat and bubbling hysterically. Krüstof cried as his cracked grin scorned his devilish sins. His mother howled forlornly as her organs fell apart into a stringy heap of crimson noodles, stained with her aortic secretions, and her greasy, bloodstained skeleton spilled gore galore. The last sounds she heard were the villainous cackles of her demented son, weeping as his demonic entertainment climaxed. And he ran. He ran from his transgression, horrified by his sociopathic pleasure. But his bloodlust subconsciously led him to his school yard, and when his classmates saw the familiar maggot lard on Krüstof's hands, they resumed their harassment. "Maggot-boy!" they chaffed, uvulas inflamed to Picassan proportions. Noyxes Tampf, Frotlim Pruniak, Rompula Daint... Had the cubes he envisioned in their fleshy throats been representative of his hard, cornered desire for acceptance?

And Krüstof killed them. He killed them all...

Krüstof loved his maggots. And now he was free, above the law, living in the unbridled woods. He was free to eat his maggots, to toss them, and they would never tease him, and no longer would the school boys and girls call him "Maggot-boy," for there were no school boys or girls anymore. Only maggots. And he loved them.

He loved one maggot more than any other. He named her Żyzny, and the normally unemotional soon-to-be-crabbo gave her his infantile heart. He cringed optimistically at her gnawing touch as she caressed his face, knowing their marriage would soon be validated. He rubbed her waxy lips and tickled her sensitive belly, which he knew confidently was what adults did for fun. A fondness in him for adults had recently manifested, for, he had noticed, they could do nearly anything with impunity, while as a child he often suffered consequences. He enforced his puckered lips upon hers with raw, violent passion, but her fragile body was not equipped to handle Krüstof's embrace. Her head exploded, her meek skull detaching easily from her rubbery spine. She died fatly against his lips, leaving crushed entrails upon his tongue.

Krüstof did not understand this death. Adults did it all the time, he knew. They never died while kissing—of this he was sure. His underdeveloped mind could not grasp that it was his ravenous roughness that had prevented their love, not Żyzny herself, and his hatred was easily identifiable upon his scarlet complexion. She hadn't accepted, he concluded. She had rather die than kiss him; for that he hated her. He loathed them all, the maggots. They were liars. They had made him this way. They were the reason he couldn't play with the schoolchildren. "Maggot-boy!" they had

139

chanted. And they were right, he thought. He was nothing but a maggot-boy.

In all his irate glory, he began to experiment with the maggots, causing them as much pain as his feeble, boyish mind could imagine. He tore them apart and sewed them back together in disgusting contortions. Thousands conglomerated into single units as he handpicked pieces from maggots that he liked and plastered them into one superior frankenmaggot. He combined hundreds of maggots in various ways into a multitude of new species, each with its own merits and, above all, weaknesses; some sizzled and writhed in pain at their genetic adjustments, while others whose experiments had better equipped them for survival, prospered with their adjustments. He placed them in great arenas with slugs upon which he happened, pitting the natural forces of good and evil against one another, and their battles, like his amusement, merited legends to describe their greatness. His love for the maggots grew newly seeded roots in his heart: Krüstof had discovered how to make maggots in whatever way he chose, and the newer, larger maggots sometimes resembled humans, which he took great pleasure in torturing.

Maggots failed to encompass the entire scope of his mutations, for he sewed multiple crab parts onto his own body, reasonably believing them to contain within them the elixir of everlasting life. He replaced his own tiny limbs with those of the crabs he fished from the foamy sea below the rocks of the plains, for, he concluded, the amount of earthly pain he would experience upon severing his limbs would be outweighed by the joy he would experience through immortality. This, he thought, was a very adult decision in which he took great pride. Through this discovery, I ascertain the falsity of the legends told of his origins, for the belief thrived that he ascended hundreds of years ago from the dark depths of the unforgiving ocean beneath our plains, and that his crabish form had insulted Mother Nature for all eternity.

So he lived, as the Zero Zone revealed, approaching more and more the fine line between monster and human, ever advancing in his mutation technologies. Some of his maggots were nearly indistinguishable from humans. One day, he thought, he would build one he could proudly call his son. For what constituted the fundamental difference between man and beast, society and chaos, civilized and primitive? There was always a fine line. Philosophers had once reasoned that the line between what is considered humane and what an atrocity to man largely blurred, and that if this line experienced sufficient foot-traffic, it would eventually disappear altogether. Krüstof had already crossed this line more times than most men did in their entire lifetimes, and his age still boasted only a single digit.

They were only two words, the two dreadful words that haunted Krüstof's innermost thoughts, that edged him over. And who could blame him?

"Maggot-boy!" they had all called. And that was all it took.

18: THE BLACK FEATHERED DEVILS

Krüstof made a name for himself before long. He became known throughout the sector as a bloodthirsty killer; no officer dared challenge him, so he lived peacefully. He was suspiciously offered a job–likely procured with snarls and other unspoken threats–as a lowly government secretary, and through the years, as his age approached the ripeness of adolescence, he ascended the ranks like a slithering tendril upon an elderly redwood. Krüstof eventually found that the opening as the Chancellor of Punishment of the sector mysteriously vanished, and he struck like an opportunistic hyena with his greatest blow yet. How he yearned for that position–what better way existed to vent his maniacal lust than to exert rightful punishment upon the wicked? So he grounded his ink and dipped his pen, for a speech promoting his position as Chancellor would soon unravel:

Krüstof sat hard in his well-worn leather office chair. Earthy, golden wrinkles lined the corners of the noble frame, and the amber undertone was as deliberately unentombèd as ever on the thoroughly battered pressure spots that generations of out-of-the-box crab thinkers and strong-jawed schemers had slouched in just the same: crustacean calf impressions, bent-over knees, long, gray, bony fingers to chin. Krüstof sighed hungrily, dreaming of the power. Youth belonged to him along with his dogged ambition. Living a life perpetually pressed for permanence, he had experienced modest highs and grave lows. He had received the worst of the world and all for nothing. At least the dead could rest. Yet he reminisced about the lifelong torture and inescapable suffering that plagued his existence, and he reflected on the true extent of the universe's wrath, with which he was not impressed. His scaly, spotted scalp twitched like a dying vermin as his cranium throbbed in deep thought.

A moist babe's tender wail softly rang throughout the dark, shadowy room. It bounced galoomphishly to the desk and danced around Krüstof's earholes. The pressure inside his head coupled with the weenieish cry pushed him to his limits, and he threw his bald, stonelike head back and flung his books to the corners of the room with a shrill roar. He kicked his tiny legs feverishly and gnawed at the air as he shrieked. The moist child's cry caught in its throat with a bubbly giggle. Krüstof inhaled and exhaled rapidly through his disfigured nose, picking up an unwanted scent of the moldy, damp, condemned room, while the cloying darkness stranded him on his own little island of dim, unexplained glow. Krüstof bellowed once more and slapped a stack of work papers down on his desk, causing other parchments and utensils to haphazardly float to the ground. His feather pens and charts caught in the wheels of his rolly chair as he awkwardly attempted to collect his things.

He returned to the stack of papers on which he worked: his speeches. They contained nothing but incomprehensible squabble and meaningless, complicated diagrams of maggots. Many of the letters were invented by Krüstof and had no respective sounds. A mind-boggling array of arrows relocated various sentences to different paragraphs and directed his eyes towards custom-made stickers reading "turn to page #(x)." None of the pages had numbers, and many were stained with strange gravies and blood from Krüstof's nose and mouth. He threw his meaty little fists down

oSpondylus Rink

on the desk in frustration. These political addresses would never win the people over.

Just when he was ready to give up, an old hermit man in a brown nappy cloak with a large hood emerged from the dark corner. He had entered uninvitedly, unbeknownst to ol' Krusty. He stiffly popped a squat square to Krüstof and gazed at him caringly.

"This is not the speech you seek. A good one would be much different. Try opening with some jokes."

Krüstof grew red with irritation as he sniveled fervently trying to locate his pen. He knew what the old man was saying was true, and he had known it himself, without any outside help. And now he looked like a fool in the presence of the respected oSpondylus Rink.

"Euggehh," murmured Krüstof. He attempted to erase the entire speech but only tore and wrinkled the page. "We'll now you've ruined my sheet. I'm going to die here. Thank you for the advice, oSpondylus," he added as he fed the old man a chocolate.

oSpondylus allowed his fetally soft skull to hang back, neck propped upright on the back of his chair. His dry lips cracked open, letting slip a curling whisp of golden vapor. He knew he was not long for this world, and Krüstof savored his imminent death, for Poseidon's disgrace could hold no candle to the aristocrat's urbane suavity, and Jealousy gnawed away at the aspiring Chancellor's maw like the vermin his reputation described. oSpondylus continued, unfazed: "And be wary, that crunching goes he who wades through pestilence. Breath fettered and polluted, catching on the cuticle membranes of dragonwings and moth pinions, he sanctions his lungs from the swarm. If his airways do not clog and swell with mucus, he will surely meet the vultures poised on the

145

purple threads of a vigile dawn. Meet he them hungry, he will leave them, indubiously glutted. Meet he them gorged, they leave him, by nature, the carnal assertor." The words escaped his parched chops like roaches scurrying from a light turned on amid their microscopic feed looting.

"And leave him the victor of the corpse they must!" speculated the young Krüstof. He had already eaten the bugs. Why not claim his tender winnings? Vulnerable as soft deli meats, the spoils of his reckless ambition lay indulgently accessible without a single predator, pack, or competing scavenger. All he had to do was carve the flesh.

"I must leave now," declared oSpondylus with aplomb as he rose. "And I'm taking the boy. Come, Wallace." He slapped at his hip, signaling the babe to follow. The ungainly, muscular infant sprang up and hurried to the departing visitor, teetering on his bare, chubby feet. With the vacuum slam of the door, directly followed by a chilling winter draft and the sleigh bells of a dry cleaners' door, came confirmation of Krüstof's lone status. He returned to his work.

19: CARNIVAL DOGS

It took Krüstof little more time to realize his bumbling inability to write effectively. The election approached in mere days, and with two drastically more experienced candidates, Trimpup Dwix and Father C24, his triumph seemed unlikely. But Krüstof had been blinded with lust, and he would stop at nothing to attain his oh-so-desired position; resorting to gruesome disembowelment of fellow candidates failed to fall beneath the crabman's morals, as would silently recount the memories of the Dwix children, whose father Krüstof sinisterly devoured.

After Krüstof took hold of the sector, Father C24's once prestigious government position was dissolved, for, as Krüstof knew, Smutny was far brighter a pupil than he, and should my new father's intellectual stimulation continue, so would expand the likelihood that he could formulate a plot to overthrow Krüstof. Father C24, Smutny Chłopak, was different from my other fathers. I loved him truly, and he lived with me for longer than any of the others. He had a sort of spirit in him—not a strong one, but more than the lackluster, soulless slaves that were my previous and later fathers. He seemed mildly aggravated by governmental oppression, unlike the quietly content bubble-boys that previously fathered me. For this reason, I always referred to Smutny merely as Father, rather than with the identification code I was technically required to use. Father earned a meager economic income, and Krüstof ascertained the suppression of his hope along with his family through planned abductions of his children. An even more devious method, however, soon replaced this torment:

A thousand suns failed to match Krüstof's rage, as villagers had become accustomed to accept. His nostrils flared dustily, for it had been years since the last infraction was committed, and his face was crackled and torn, yearning for lotion or other natural oils to sleeken his uneven facial rifts. Smutny Chłopak plopped his weary body down brutishly. His primal desires surpassed those of all his brethren, for no other had ever dared confront Krüstof on the grounds that life proved too inhospitable to bear.

Smutny had been placed in the Intereducational Correction Facility three years ago. Year one provided a beautifully poetic film account of his past year of life. He watched interestedly, for Krüstof had wisely recorded Smutny's entire year so that Smutny could observe himself making mistakes, so as to avoid them in the future. Smutny wept as he saw himself with his children. How he yearned to see us more; but work was work, and Krüstof needed it done properly. So Smutny had accepted one year in the Facility, for if it would motivate more efficient progress in the future, it would have been a sensible investment.

He sat uncomfortably upon a plank of asphalt with jagged metal cuffs restraining his wrists. He saw himself through thick and thin, through sleep and through the rarity of feeding, and he remembered every embarrassing detail vividly. He often dozed off during the less action-packed moments; the eye-clamps did their duties, however: his eyes constantly creaked forcibly open at the hands of the metallic tweezers, grinding mechanically, piercing his bleeding eyelids. They wrenched his corneas into consciousness, and every few hours, when the lack of blinking greedily sucked the moisture out of his eyes, turning them into a vast, salty, crusty

148

desert, the clamps would secrete a maggot-juice spray to hydrate Smutny's seelookers. From this desolate, ocular wasteland, with boiling fissures and festering blisters, with sautéed blemishes and vascular boils, with rank fungi and sandy terraces, would supposedly flower a soggy swampland of fertile visionary capability. The oils aroused insufferable pain, but, after a handful of doses, the brain would learn to suicidally sever those nerves. Consequently, Smutny accomplished no sleep that year, but he quietly accepted his fate with the false impression that he would return to his home upon the New Year's dawn. And the next year came.

Krüstof proposed that Smutny stay a few more days, just to see himself watching himself for a small while. It would be interesting, Krüstof insisted, to see his reaction to various clips in the film. And time passed. Days rolled into weeks, which disguised themselves as months, which revealed themselves to be years. Two years of this passed—of Smutny watching himself watch footage of himself. The paradox grew with the years, with no time to think of a way to escape the madness, for there always remained footage to be watched, since the cameras rolled for all 365 days of the year, and it therefore took exactly 365 days to watch all of the year's footage.

Now Smutny stood before Krüstof, wasting valuable educational time that he could have used to watch more footage, begging for return to his home. And Krüstof beat him with his claws—beat him within an inch of death—and sentenced him to a lifetime of work on the ash farms. This was, as Smutny understood, a just and gracious sentence for such a severe infraction: the infraction of questioning one's fate, as the Chancellor claimed.

149

Through this punishment, Krüstof kept Father from my family. We were without money for years, for women and children were prohibited to work for wages, although illegal, unpaid labor persisted by expressed consent and demand on the part of the very government that banned the labor in the first place. It would be another year before Krüstof would show Smutny mercy, allowing him to work on the maggot farms rather than those that vainly and toxically attempted to organically produce the skin of volcanoes (Krüstof rated volcanoes as the mark of a truly cool aristocrat, deciding that his mansion should be decorated accordingly–with a blanket of soot). I tried to explain to Father the evil of Krüstof. After all, had it not been for my nautical nemesis, Father would rule the sector. But my father had been brainwashed, for he felt only gratitude at Krüstof's mercy, for, as he claimed, he had committed an unpardonable offense.

He once wrote a letter to his own assigned father–a letter that never graced the hand of the recipient due to the eventual residence of all mail in the Chancellor's stomach–describing his current state. The letter read as follows:

"My sons have not seen me in years. They would not recognize me now, for my once youthful essence and cheerful optimism has been crudely replaced with vulgar scars of chastised abuse. My nose is pulverized to a semisolid fecal sack, my cheeks gaunt and hollow, my eyes sadly bewildered. The eyes of a man with no hope–a man who has lost everything at the hands of a cruel dictator. The cloudy pupils of despair, the bloodshot veins of insomnia…

Yes, I once rode the refined vehicle of a valiant youth. But now I am Krüstof's example to the people. I toil endlessly on the maggot farms, my only menial task to whip the maggocattle. They moo sluggishly, inching across the pasture with oblivious delight. Krüstof milks them often, but their excretions are nothing more than murky maggot meat. Only the fittest provide high protein, and it is therefore required to whip them constantly to test their skeletal support.

Those that are weak or fetal are torn to shreds and leave behind convulsing remains in the face of death. Their viscous juices stain clothes permanently, and the unbearable stench dissolves the fibers immediately.

Those that are strong enough to survive the attack are even worse in that their adamantine shells reflect the whip's blow. It bounces off them and lacerates my face, so when a maggot is whipped I pray sincerely that it will be weak, for a few ruined clothes are no consequence compared to a bleeding incision.

And so I live, my only sustenance the rotting corpses of dead maggots, my only penance the pardon of my infraction by the government, for which I am eternally grateful."

Krüstof's punishment surpassed traditional cruelty. He stripped the spirit from a once great man, convincing him that lawful justice had merely taken its course. Krüstof often remembered Smutny's plea to work in a different department, and the mere thought of an individual having control over his own life, rather than Krüstof himself, made his face contort in anger and confusion. He screamed often, distraught at what he saw as an attempted rebellion. Krüstof decided that his mercy would be short lived, and he would again punish Smutny, more severely than ever before:

Krüstof sneered. He lobbed his handsome fists grievously at a perforated Smutny, scolding him infinitely for his offense. Smutny smiled meekly as Krüstof ground his skull to a puddingy yolk. It blooped and babbled like a sediment-rich brook, leaching vital knuckular minerals into the brain osmotically, but providing no cranial resistance. Though Krüstof's crabby fists tenderized Smutny's vulnerable grey matter, Smutny could not help but chuckle loftily, for his life had been pardoned, and it was only natural for Krüstof to expel his seething fury. Wisps of lukewarm pus trickled slobbishly down Smutny's bruised, bumpy scalp. Festering sores sprouted after each blow Krüstof lugged upon the skull, bleeding in chunky clots as Smutny's tenderized muscles receded from the point of impact, fearing the sting of the corpulent punisher, fleeing as cowards from their moral duty of protecting the brain.

The skull gave way easily enough. Bits of serrated bone jaggedly punctured Krüstof's knuckles, but his adrenaline surged, and he felt nothing. Smutny sobbed quietly, shamed by his crime and thankful for his merciful punishment as Krüstof groped his naked brain. It stank. The bubbling odor floated intrusively into Krüstof's nostrils, crawling carefully among boogery caverns and into his nasal abyss. Krüstof grimaced, and the smell made him angry. He suddenly hated Smutny for this rank stench, cursing him for causing his nose to scrunch whimperingly.

And he held Smutny's brain, his life in his hands, and prepared to murder as he had done so many times before, until his fingers delved into the meaty organ, and he found comfort in the familiar maggoty texture. He squished chunks of the brain and smeared them on his cheeks, and he chortled. The pink lard coated his palms, and he remembered vividly the days of his youth when he had loved the maggots so. They were his only friends, and he cringed at the somber thought that this friendship had come to a bitter close. Tears streamed down oily cheeks. He played with the brain just as if it had been the maggots he once adored. He tossed handfuls of it into the air, chewed on some, and rubbed himself with them, laughing maniacally. He remembered all these joyful activities, and he yearned for reconciliation with his tiny companions.

But alas, the fat on his hands reminded him of something else: the brutal teasing that the maggots had entailed. Of the endless mockery he had endured, the cruel children hating his favorite things and embarrassing him for his oddity.

"Maggot-boy!" They had called him. He looked down in horror at Smutny's still lips, and in his mind he invented a scenario in which Smutny had uttered these two despicable words—the two words with which his classmates had so often mocked him, these two words of hate and ostracism.

"Maggot-boy!" Smutny called. Of course, Smutny said nothing, and his quiet, stern face resembled one of pure destinal acceptance. "Maggot-boy!" Krüstof imagined. No amount of hatred could have matched that of Krüstof then, for he could not believe that this transgressor would dare scorn his authority.

Krüstof wailed violently, screaming in profanity as his fists rained a barrage of horrendous strikes deep into Smutny's custardy brain. Smutny said nothing, and this enraged Krüstof further, for he

153

knew Smutny would not rebel to this beating, so he unleashed a beast of anger upon Smutny, relieving built-up fury from his elementary years. His hatred was a taunted circus lion, caged sinisterly, and finally the cage had been unlocked, and the beast was free to roam once more, to slaughter and to gorge on the blood of its enemies, to reign supreme as it instinctively desired, to eat heavily as it once had, to put an end to its insatiable appetite. He voraciously pulverized Smutny's limp head, pulping and juicing his sinewy grey matter, stringing apart individual muscles with gross carelessness and infatuated negligence. His claws blurred, frenziedly chomping Smutny's wounded flesh.

Hours passed. Smutny fluctuated between this world and the next. He clung to life like a masticated vine to a weakening oak. Finally, Krüstof's blind fury dissipated entirely, and Smutny felt the warm relief of the final pints of blood rolling hotly down his nose and forehead. Krüstof ran his fingers through the blackish liquid, gradually feeling his way into Smutny's eyes. He jostled them out of his way, opening the fjord of Smutny's eye socket and clasping his loose skin. He felt the faint grip of a disheveled man, and, quivering in terror, he plunged his entire arm into Smutny's head. He needed to save the man trapped within Smutny's face! Oooo!

Reaching deeper into the skull, finally confirming his suspicion, he locked hands with a clearly cadaverous figure, whose fingers were surrounded by only a ragged canvas of baggy skin but no muscles or ligaments. He pulled the man out, and to his astonishment the man held the hand of a corpulent woman, who attached to yet a third figure. So they came out of Smutny's watery head, one by one, each linked to two others, holding hands carefully

154

like a paper people chain. And Krüstof startled in fright, for they were members of his family—all people whose lives he had extinguished, all blood relatives. His visage contorted in shame; he knew he had sinned. They looked at him flatly and monotonously chanted "Maggot-boy!" in ominous unison. Krüstof cursed the gods, he cursed Smutny, and he cursed the maggots.

Historians now know that this did not happen, for this is impossible. Krüstof did not find his family within Smutny. Instead, he found something much worse. As Krüstof absentmindedly pulled Smutny's stretchy skin off his head, a different man stared back into his eyes. The man had the grey eyes of a killer, unfeeling and stoic, hard and oppressed. His cheeks were warm and lumpy, his lips parched drily. He sneered treacherously, conniving a murderous plot as always. The man staring back into Krüstof's eyes was a mirror, for he and Krüstof were one and the same.

Krüstof's face contorted in disbelief and utter confusion; the man shackled in the chair before him was not Smutny after all, but Krüstof. The Krüstof in the chair smirked wildly as he gripped his gun, and his bullet pierced the standing Krüstof's heart. Insane and bewildered, bleeding and dying, Krüstof stared at his killer. He toppled over flaccidly, flopping onto the bloody floor like a wet noodle. The surviving Krüstof, cackling in his chair, examined the empty room.

There rested no blood on the floor, nor Smutny Chłopak, who, Krüstof now remembered, had never entered the building in the first place. Nor did there exist a dead man, for the bullet Krüstof had shot never went through a body. The man it had killed was an illusion: the personification of Krüstof's hatred—a figment of his own imagination. In his expulsion of his repressed anguish, he unleashed his evil, and a softer Krüstof emerged as consequence– one capable of love and affection, and one who would reconcile with his much missed maggots. Should he truly have been a wormchild, his evil brethren would silently have condemned his newfound benevolence. But this transformation was not impeccable, for he would sin again. It would not be long before Krüstof would decide to kill Smutny anyways for the rude remarks he had made during Krüstof's hallucination. Thus, the Chancellor set off to find Smutny, and murder swiftly resurfaced to Krüstof's malevolent character; never again would I look upon the only fathe I ever loved...

20: THE UNACCUSTOMED ASTRONAUT

Cowardice drives men more than ambition, and fear prevents more than even death. Krüstof remained wary of Smutny's corpse, praying to himself that my deceased father—one of only two men who aroused envy within him (oSpondylus Rink had once exerted this very effect on the crabman, but his civilized, chivalric disposition, as a direct result of contrast with Krüstof's political authority, which his mental supercomputer failed to comprehend, automatically teleported the distinguished aristocrat to a more suiting dimension)—would not attempt to usurp his now-Chancelloric government position. But Krüstof's thirst for suffering and torture remained far from quenched, and he began to exert his power murderously so as to avoid challenges to his rule by iron, softshell fist. His regulations discriminated against every class of man, leaving all oppressed victims to wade in the black liquid of prejudice. Among these regulations were those regarding the overweight, which had interstellar consequences:

The fervent skitter approached the rocketry lab with inevitable determination. As the click-clacking gradually amplified, the chubber's forced breath exponentially shortened. He inhaled and exhaled so rapidly that he began to suffocate, and he could feel the stuffed pleather restraints constricting his blood flow. Finally, after what seemed like hours, the obtuse crust-lord made his entrance. Young, promising, Caucasian male scientists in white lab coats dove to the hard, unwavering floor to clear minuscule mess from Krüstof's path. He did not hesitate or yield. Krüstof used their feeble vertebrae as stepping stones for his stern, rocklike, mollusk legs. His pointy toes smashed their ribcages to dust and penetrated

157

their tender organs, leaving a warm human broth with croutons aplenty. The moist crunch of their spines crushing filled the ears of an irrelevant hag; she will not be addressed again, for she is extraneous. The bloodsoaked pincers screeched on the white-flecked tile as the brobdingnagian crab man halted at his captive's stocks.

"You have violated USSR Public Fortune Regulations, amendment 617D. The policy clearly states that being fat is illegal," growled the morbidly obese tyrant in disgust. His assorted chins rippled with every word, and his righteous chops wagged in agreement. "In violating this policy, you have automatically volunteered your body to science. You will be launched from right here on earth and sent into orbit with a camera strapped to your head. Glorious isn't it? Quite the sacrifice you have made. So generous to your comrades," he muttered. His words poured from his overstuffed maw like gravy from a roasted turkeys anüs, and the mere thought of Krüstof's corpulence deeply revolted even "tuff" men almost as much as did his hypocrisy. The poor devil in shackles wriggled feverishly, but to no avail.

"We thank you sincerely," spat the barnacle-ridden, haughty grandeur as he swiftly turned on his beshellèd heels, toppling a lab cart with his unhealthily plump loins. The captive's violent screams were muffled by his limited edition Mag-o-Gag. Ethnically assorted rocket engineers and fuel scientists converged on his tilted cot restraint and lowered it to table level. They strapped a large video camera to his forehead and bestowed a two-way headset onto his thrashing scalp. One clean-cut young man leaned over his face and announced: "YOU WILL NOT BE SENT INTO ORBIT. RECORD SPACE FOR ETERNITY. SIGN HERE."

A capped pen was stuffed into the chubber's clammy hand, and a forged document with his signature was unceremoniously presented by another rocketeer. They hastily wheeled him over to the launch pad and rammed the cot into the flight pod. The contraption began steaming, and a shrill honking commenced; the ceiling retracted, revealing the clear, silently whistling sky. The pod blasted ferociously into the unknown, and the political prisoner's lardy frame whistled through the air atop the metal cot. Justice was done.

21: Born Of Blue Whales

Despite his reputation as the most cold-blooded crustacean in all of Christendom, Chrysanthemum, and Chronos, challenges to his governmental throne did indeed arise. On the fateful night of Baron Grosslefrond's hat-expansion party, a cosmic omen rocketed into Krüstof's world like a furious meteor. During his second mug of unpasteurized swine milk, Krüstof ripped off his eyebrows and chucked them into the air, his expression demonstrating the highest surprise. His alarm had been triggered by the reports of the Kraba Observatory stewards; a galactic rainbow had been spotted, and the source likely resided on the nearest beach, per educated estimation. The observatory steward delivered this message to Krüstof with the utmost urgency yet through a strained whisper so as to not disturb the nobles attending the ceremony; unfortunately, his efforts were squandered as his wide eyes and imperative demeanor immediately hushed the entire congregation.

"THE COSMIC RAINBOW...?" hissed Krüstof through clenched teeth as if the prismatic plasma lanyard itself had wired his jaw shut.

"AFFIRMATIVE SIR... And our rainbow remote appears to be somehow... not working?" replied the young steward.

Dumbfounded at the failure of his useless gizmo, Krüstof barely had time to take another hearty swig of the watery, curdled teet juice before completing his second spit take directly onto Baron Grosslefrond's non-amphibious mistress (interracial relationships were trending in the advanced society of the modern elite). Krüstof swatted his ceramic mug clean off the table with one swift backhand and leapt from his chair, tipping it behind him, and Baron

Grosslefrond threw his head back in shock as his throat inflated like an airbag.

But the steward was unfinished. There was another pressing matter at hand.

"AND SIR, there is one more problem. A little furry creature has come to the door with a package. It claims it is for you."

"A... creature?"

"AFFIRMATIVE. It claims to be... a king."

At this Krüstof sneered, confident in his own status as the sole ruler of everything. Expecting to assassinate the wannabe immediately, he made a condescending face and motioned with an accepting gesture that sent the steward sprinting out of the room.

Krüstof was still chuckling faintly to himself when the door slammed shut and the soft patter of paws against the porcelain floors intensified until coming to an abrupt halt. Before the Chancellor could finger his holster for his weapon, the mammalian creature crawled up Krüstof's legs and stomach and leapt onto the table. In an impressively coordinated display, the creature swung its strange cargo forward with one arm and lifted the opposite foot as it did so, twirling gracefully and dangling its package over its head. It suddenly planted its raised foot firmly downwards while simultaneously joining both hands together in a powerful grasp upon the mass that it carried, and as it finally unclenched its pupils and tilted up its chin to meet the stunned Chancellor's uncomprehending gaze, it slammed the strange bulk against the tabletop. The liquids shuddered in their glasses and reverberated gradually to a standstill as Krüstof attempted to understand what had occurred.

In an athletic stance before him was an otter king, and in its hand was a root baby. It released its grip from the whimpering babe carefully, so as not to spook the skeptical Chancellor, before taking two long strides backwards. The steward had only then caught up to the swift otter king and rushed onto the scene, but he stopped when he noticed the silence and observed the delicacy of the situation at hand. All the guests, too, were unnerved and motionless.

After a brief pause, Krüstof slowly cupped his claws around the tender root baby, massaging its skin and exploring its consistency. He looked up at the otter king for approval, and when the king nodded softly, the Chancellor raised the baby over his head in triumph. This was his baby. It instantaneously became his everything—the culmination of all his dedicated hard work and precise paternal instincts. He poured every ounce of his being into loving the beautiful creature that was now so satisfactorily his, and his face quivered with muscular contortions as he pioneered new emotions that had never been felt before by anyone, for they were far too powerful to be contained by anyone else.

"You… are… MINE!" he shrieked as he stared the baby in the face with a lunatic grin. The guests were unsure of the proper response, and a couple attempted to initiate a round of applause, though they only succeeded in a few stray, unconnected claps.

The steward piped up:

"Sir, don't you–" his rude interjection was interrupted by a bullet tearing through his brain. The root baby, which Krüstof had unintentionally let go to grab his pistol, crashed against the hard ground and cracked slightly open. Krüstof examined the agonized baby for a long moment as it writhed in pain and released small cries that floated through the air in glum pockets. The emotive pendulum of a Chancellor stomped on the root baby without much of a thought, destroying its skull with an evil finality. He cleared the smoke from the barrel of his weapon with an assertive blow, and the otter king crawled up his back to perch itself proudly on his shoulder.

"Well then. Let's go find this rainbow," he offered.

Minutes later, a small coastguard caravan accompanied by local astronomers trundled down the weedy beach, leaving perfect tire tracks in the untouched sand as it rolled along, until it approached the last dune separating them from the source of the mystical phenomenon. Krüstof's personal unit of guards hopped off the foremost jeep and aimed down the sights of their rifles. Scientists from the observatory hustled towards the first vehicle.

Krüstof slung the door of his transport open with considerable force and rolled out onto the beach. He arose from the damp sand looking like an indignified breaded cutlet. He waddled as fast as his little legs would carry him to the top of the dune, hell-bent on being the first to see the mysterious spectacle. He sprinted at an astonishingly low speed past a lab nerd holding a clipboard, shoving him onto the beach as he went, submerging him in his ephemeral watery grave. Krüstof's corpulent frame emerged like a burst maraschino cherry from behind the summit of the whipped, creamlike dune. Being the fastest man on the planet was sweet. Less sweet, however, was the unsavory origin of the organic lightshow that terrified his regime that night. It was corpulent, and indeed, it was not sweet.

163

Krüstof squatted low as he gasped like his soul was vacuumed from his throat by an electric shaman. He was horrified to discover that the source of the rainbow was the reflection of the jewels encrusted on a most magnificent narwhal that had washed up on his shore. It was the longest and most muscular narwhal anyone had ever seen, except for one man, because he, to his children's dismay, could not see.

FACTOID: This man was blind.

BONUS FACTOID: This man could not provide for his children. They are dead now.

The majestic beast reared its head, dicing the tension in the air around him with his gleaming tusk, conjuring a serene aura of tranquility that imbibed the malignant aggression cleanly out of the sacrosanct crabman and replaced it with a curiously aroused awe and admiration. Krüstof immediately suppressed this tremor of respect with an aggravated grunt and an uncoordinated agglomeration of wild swats. He jerked his head back and threw adirectional punches until he tumbled down the sand dune. His assistants rushed to his side in attempt to pull the elephantine arthropod to his feet but were violently shooed away, their tracheas blackened not only with bruises but also with residual soot from 'Stof's ashy fists.

"NO, NO, NO!!!" Krüstof howled, personally offended by the political threat of another nautical specimen dwelling amongst the civilians of Grunty Kraba. His own men could not see him like this, openly challenged and bereft of an intelligent parry. Mesmerized by the ocean mammal's noble pulchritude, Krüstof knew he could not win, but this had never been reason enough for him to lose. Krüstof could not be made a fool of without dire consequences, and, not wishing to be triumphed any further, he condemned the venerable ocean steed to be cast into the hyperborean tundra of Norstrindain, where the desolate hellscape of singing ice and teasingly inadequate sunlight glared over the destitute horizon, mocking those unfortunate enough to wish to bask, and where arctic winds swept over the devoid wasteland, whipping the hide of forsaken travelers, whispering Perish Songs–morbid lullabies never to be recanted to those nestled in the warm bosom of climates above absolute zero–to them in their last hours. None knew just how deep the ice's blistering toes crept, or exactly how far North it sprawled, but it did not matter to the indignant chancellor, who insisted none of his employees sleep until the aquatic fiend of his nightmares be cast off into arctic oblivion.

Soon after his typically dictatorial orders, a fleet of helicopters departed from the closest airport, hauling the narwhal in a net suspended several yards under the central chopper. Packed with space heaters, nuclear microwave guns, artificial fire supplies, and burly airmen bundled to the teeth, the airborne armada swiftly disappeared over the edge of the world. Just as the narwhal unshaped into a tiny black dot hanging from another, a jewel on its breastplate glinted like a laser into Krüstof's eyes, momentarily blinding him, or perhaps only catching his attention for a moment to bid him adieu. "Until next time, my Krusty," it suggested.

The waters rose several inches within the next few days–a true testament to the massiveness of the banished creature–but the extent of habitability of Gruntian lands and the nutritional value of the fruits they produced seemed to be augmented substantially, as if

165

the narwhal had died so much that other life had to spontaneously generate in order to restore universal balance.

22: THE TRAGEDY OF THE BUNKER BABIES

As the posse of political elite followed their Chancellor on a customary stroll through the villages, Krüstof leered in disgust at the underwhelming performance of the local incinerator decorations. This week, the participants had exhibited extraordinarily terrible artistic capabilities, even more unappealing than usual, and by the time he had failed six neighborhood entries, he had just about had it. All the while, wrapped around the Chancellor's sacred waist rested a familiar monarch: the dreaded otter king I had encountered with Yuelfrik in the river. It wore a necklace laced with bark, dead fish, child toys, and severed fingers, and its gaze swept the horizon in scrutiny, seemingly searching for any object eye-catching enough to merit its seizure. The menacing, demanding congregation dragged along the ground a weighty shadow whose gravity pulled all darkness towards it and left its surroundings entirely swallowed by unbearable light.

Krüstof wiped the stale puke from his mouth while one of his pupils disobediently strayed from his desired field of vision to instead deliver unto him the foulest sight of the contest thus far: a weirdly painted artistic abomination with overly-simplified geometry and incorrect coloration. The nervous competitors forced smiles and twiddled their fingers as the Chancellor bestowed unto their creation a look of mild discontent, discomfort, and indigestion. He rose his gaze to meet the eyes of one man before disapprovingly shaking his head back and forth and wagged his mocking finger in musical rejection. He shook that head of his.

"No, no, no," he cooed.

One shake no, shake two no, and-a-no-and-a-three. This did not bode well.

"It's modern art!" the man stammered in a sweat. "It's supposed to look like that."

The otter king raised his little paws to Krüstof's ear without unlocking his pupil's accusing stare from the man's terrified visage. Krüstof, who also remained intensely focused on the man as the king babbled on, rose both eyebrows in moderate intrigue, yet his eyelids did not budge from their indifferent positioning just below halfway up his eyeballs. When the otter king finally released his hold on the Chancellor's ear, Krüstof took his time to breathe, unintentionally inhaling the nauseating aroma of the man's steamy bowels. Finally, Krüstof casually touched his thumb to one side of his neck before gradually, unhurriedly dragging it across his throat to the other side. Two guards behind him stepped forward and grasped the man's arms to lug him to the incinerator. The rest of the competitors who had also participated in these distasteful decorations were denied so valiant a death—the otter king climbed up their torsos and ripped out their throats with his teeth.

In the midst of the screams, Krüstof stomped on the toes of a spectating father with two children in his arms, and the king scurried up the Chancellor's back and cupped his adorable little paws against Krüstof's ear. After intently listening to the king's whisperings, Krüstof looked forcefully at the father, pointed at the baby on his left shoulder, and motioned towards himself with his bony claw. The otter king crossed his arms as he impatiently awaited the transaction to be completed, and after substantial struggling and the threat of a wet-willy, the father tearfully relinquished one of his children. Perking up in excitement, the otter king happily received the young child and leapt off Krüstof's shoulder, awkwardly shuffling into the water before swimming skillfully away and out of sight with its precious cargo.

Just then, one of the guards in the group, an incredibly important art representative for whom Krüstof had great respect, budded in.

"After detailed analysis, I have concluded that these decorations are in fact judged by all of art to be excellent. The attention to simplicity is astounding. It demonstrates commendable passion and initiative. Bravo to these gentlemen. An absolute delight!"

Krüstof stared blankly at the art representative for several seconds as he processed the artistic verdict. After brief consideration, he too declared the decorations of the dead men to be of the finest aesthetic quality. He pulled the trophy–a barrel of maggots, as always–he had prepared for the winning neighborhood out from his back pocket.

"These guys are the best," he carelessly reported. With one hand, he tossed the trophy onto the ground, and the maggots spilled over one of the bleeding bodies. The congregation stared at the mess for a moment until Krüstof finally broke the silence. "They will be given a proper funeral. Tomorrow at dawn. Someone bring a toy for me to play with."

All who attended the funeral were promptly executed for leaving their posts during hours of labor without authorization.

23: THE STREETS THAT SCREAMED

Krüstof was unfortunately not only corrupted with his absolute authority, but also by his own psyche; his deranged, obscured conscience became a contorted shell of its former moral self. He snickered maniacally, tearing his vocal cords as he shrieked and flailed his arms like a climaxing lunatic. His already worrisome hysteria exponentially augmented as he browsed the photographed progress of sinister human experimentation that he had ordered. He had the whole process scrapbooked, and, one had to admit, the borders he used around the photos were too cute!

A former comrade of his, with whom he fought side-by-side for the glory of the Soviet Union, was called upon to tamper with and edit the foundations of human genetics. Krüstof paid generous salary to provide a comfortable, luxurious stay for his friend, Yægelshmick, a man of scientific credibility. Officer Yægelshmick developed formulas for harsh chemical solutions with which he treated the human skin, attempting, upon the Chancellor's demand, to transmutate humans into scientifically altered creatures roughly resembling maggots for Krüstof's personal entertainment. He applied various scarring chemicals that fizzed and popped as they melted away at the skins of the unfortunate victims. The screams of the patients escaped the chambers beneath the streets, and I still remember trembling in my bed as the demented howls ransacked my auditory canals. Yægelshmick surgically implanted strange mucus glands to keep the skin moist and smooth, but the unsanitary surgical cuts he proudly made became infected, and his patients died with amputated limbs and swollen nubs. Their skin was instead

171

scabby and scaly, laced with patches of blisters that appeared as green orbs radiating a radioactive glimmer.

Failure condemned the experiments. Soon, Yægelshmick could not prolong his stay in our village, and his secret patients were tossed out onto the streets, most already deceased, dispatched by chemical burns. He forcibly continued his research as he traveled with his squadron across the Soviet Provinces. Most of the land was war-torn and useless, leaving the provinces in constant turmoil; battles perpetually surged, for although the Soviet Union dominated the known universe, its political consistency was meek and tenuous. Territorial disputes raged frequently within the loosey-goosey confederation, and war campaigns emerged as suddenly as they dissipated. Yægelshmick and his men served well to the stronger of two provinces in one such territorial skirmish, leading to their temporary release of duty, and a cease-fire had nearly manifested into a peace treaty by the time 'Shmick's humano-maggot research had commenced. Despite imminent peace, Yægelshmick's commander ordered his squadron to crush any minor opposition left in the rebelling countryside as they moved toward Yægelshmick's private laboratory under our city; projections by the elite Gruntian mathematicians estimated that his return to our village would take place simultaneously with the termination of his military service in approximately 45, after which his focus on human experimentation would resume.

One fateful day however, his convoy of armored vehicles crossed an uncharted field in attempt to avoid northern conflicts. The trucks veered off the dirt road and strayed into the long grasses of the ominous barren lands, but the eerie quiet failed to generate anxiety amongst the platoon, for the field was believed to be inactive–a fatal miscommunication. This field in fact remained juicily poised for execution of its mechanical orders, and his truck exploded as the front tire detonated an unforeseen mine. The truck flipped and rolled as it tumbled across the fields in a violent flash of flame and a badass burst of metal. The fire spilled across the snowy fields.

Yægelshmick, the only survivor, observed the molten muscles and blood of his companions slapped against the steering wheel. The explosion severed his legs, hidden beneath the rubble of his van, which had been reduced to ash and scrap metals. He pulled himself across the remainder of the field with his arms, clawing at the ground in awe of his misfortune. His skin simmered away, melting off his bones like wax. As he reached the side of the road, he frosted over, one arm gripping the dirt and the other tragically extended, and his skin froze mid-drip while rippling off of his body. A small frozen puddle of his own skin surrounded him, and this is how the peasant children of the Snail District discovered him the next week as they marched to their snail farms.

They gave him a proper funeral. Krüstof had been invited, but his bitter attitude towards his old companion, derived from Yægelshmick's failure to properly conduct the experiments he had desired, drove him away from the event. He prevented all from attending the service, including Yægelshmick's family, with failure to cooperate punishable by death. The funeral hall boasted maximum vacancy, for Krüstof's resentment had been volatile, and he yearned for the plagues of sorrow and misery to taint Yægelshmick's afterlife. But his crime had been greater than this, for he had known

173

all along that the fatal field of Yægelshmick's demise to which he ordered the officer had yet to be cleared.

One can try to change a man, but evil is deep rooted, and once it has taken residence, it can never be killed. Evil can only be cut from the stem, but it will regenerate. Visionaries will live ignorantly, blissfully unaware of the misconducts of society, investing their faith into the good of man. All men are tainted and call the wise cynical for wielding this truth, but they are the realists.

24: Stone Asylum

The animosity between Krüstof and the Chłopak family had become increasingly clear. It had not been long since his murder of Father before he began to target me. Krüstof resented my existence, and rightfully so; it was none but my hand that had crushed his beloved automobile, none but my father who had doubted his omniscience, none but my brother who had destroyed his home. Krüstof sought to destroy all evidence of the Chłopak family's existence, and if he succeeded in killing me as he had to so many of my siblings, he would finally have cleansed the world of our bloodline. His thirst childishly enticed his attack as he uncontrollably salivated for a chance to exterminate me, which, he thought, should be no difficult task, as his experience dwarfed that of any killer. And so he came.

His supernatural strength made carrying the squeaky-clean, recently renovated silo a metaphorical breeze. It must have carried billions of ordinary maggots and any number of mutant creations. Two meaty, clunky legs rasped against the wiggly sack that formed the back of the maggohound that he rode—majestic but incredibly inefficient. The hound dragged its agonized belly across the coarse earth, bleeding and crying in pain; its existence was never meant to be, and its soul begged to be destroyed by a negligent God, who failed to understand how it lived without His consent, for it was no member of His divine plan and no spawn of His masterful fingertips.

Krüstof crept slowly towards me, smirking triumphantly. He had conquered yet another realm: the art of life. I imagined him painting life across a graveyard, spilling biology into corpses long enskeleted. He would sculpt passion into those dead eyes, pruning

175

the gray clumps of excess clay. But he could not revive those who had never died–those gray, rotted eyes of the lifeless living... No, his creation was by no means perfect, but it was beautiful, even seductive in his eyes, so he took no notice of the beast's excruciating pleas for death. He rode to my home in the shoes of God Himself; now that he boasted a successful mutant maggot, both Krüstof and the villagers knew that a god was no longer necessary. Krüstof had conquered Him and assumed His duty of creating life, and his deformed mascot provided living proof, though anyone could tell the beast's life would end soon, for none can defy the will of Mother Nature for eternity, and she would soon rectify the injustice that had been served upon her. The unnatural, anatomically illegal maggohound stared her defiantly in the eyes and mocked her, teasing her momentary lapse of control, chuckling at its victory over the divine forces. But this manipulation and ultimate surpassing of nature further enraged the elemental forces, and Mother Nature would await the correct time to enact her unrelenting revenge against man. Because from the dawn of man's creation, there has existed firm palisade from the wild. This barrier had sculpted man from the creatures of the earth. Now God's power rested in the incompetent claws of a mortal being–a being that Mother Nature could devour with one blink of an eye. She becomes the grand overseer, and her authority can no longer be curbed by the forces of her own creator. Her jurisdiction is decided in the wild calculus of the jungle. It alone will reign supreme.

Having expected Krüstof to slap me with the hairy palm of havoc, I had prepared my house ahead of time: it was solid concrete. The substance densely packed the entire home, the coarse rocks providing excellent maggot resistance. A hole, perfectly centered, provided for my residence. It followed the exact contours of my adolescent form so accurately that concretal residue obediently filled every hole in my body. Mouth, ears, nose, belly button, etcetera: all plugged. My pores proved no exception, clogged as snugly as Krüstof's severely undersized toilet. Only my Mag-o-Gag provided the jaunty sweetness of fresh air necessary to survive the night, tainted only partially by the rank of the squirming maggots within.

My garage door had been replaced with a tunnel, drainable at the touch of a button. While open, the treacherous tunnel depicted millions of frames of my body, posing in slightly different positions. The porcupinal walls and rigorous transitions made escape or entry impossible without the infinite knowledge I possessed of its endless, prismatic booby traps. The sirenic lure of the Larwamorphic pathways would entrap intruders in a cemental prison, while my muscle memory allowed me to transverse the hallway utilizing my impractically high acrobatic agility. At my verbal command, the hall would fill in with liquid maggo-cement—an unimaginably terrible substance. Upon this release, the hallway's leaking pores would swell and infect pussily, farting loudly, tartar seeping from every crevice. The cement would scream loudly like a man who contagiously coughed ebolous phlegm. But it was a necessary evil, for no matter the weaknesses, maggo-cement provided one vital advantage: it could melt upon the introduction of electric current, as confirmed by four very tall scientists. Thus, upon my awakening, the cement would drip cleanly out, draining through a series of tubes and pipes guiding it to a tank atop the house, where it would recycle back to refill the hallway after having allowed my escape through the vacant tunnel. This process I repeated daily, and since none had yet dared to commit the infraction of home individualization—all bungalows were two-walled holes in the earth equipped with a poophole and a multipurpose barrel—Krüstof did not expect his plan to fail.

His feeble crustacean mind could not compute any possible error with his simpleton plot, for he had crafted incredibly precise blueprints. These blueprints proved unlike the many other official documents that he scribbled down in crayon, the crooked letters skewed by the arthritis reverb rattling through his shell; no, thousands of sheets illustrated his kindergarten-level plan, all at different angles, and all with various annotations. He had calculated the margin of error to be zero percent. Top mathematicians spent days huddled together in a room with chalkboard walls, no provisions but their calculators and their formulas—all of the world's brilliant minds brought under one roof only to check his arithmetic repeatedly. It was a one step plan, depicted by a childish yet neat drawing of my house, accompanied by a crudely sketched stick man, who must have been Krüstof, depicted with his multitude of legs and an arrow aiming from the latter to the former. The third, undrawn factor: the maggots. They were plentiful, and hungry of course.

The plan decreed that the maggots would devour me. I would pay for my family's infraction, and Krüstof would be a hero. He had done well, he thought. I perhaps thought similarly. Perhaps a family of minority had no right to make the distinction of right and wrong. And perhaps I would be OATMEAL for the FLIES!

His associates would envy him. They would be impressed at his bountiful wisdom, his intricate cleverness, his deft cunning. Satisfied with the finished stack of papers in hand, he had jittered as the date of execution crept across the calendar, closer and closer, and he wept away with merry tears, weeping, to find bliss with the thought that he reiterated as he wept–weeping, mind you–that he would finally be revered. He would be a hero. A hero who wept.

This I let him believe as he gaily galloped to my home haunched with his polished maggot silo on back, salivating grinchously for his caramel vengeance. He threw the silo, slamming it with an elephant's stark girth and a toddler's accuracy. The projectile almost veered off with the eastern winds–winds that carried the tune of some strange beast, if I may add (You may not.). His fetal delight at the destruction for which he bore responsibility radiated pity. He squealed ecstatically, jeered wildly and farted accidentally as he bent his knees and touched four fingers to his lips. He felt embarrassed.

The maggots had become energized. Their approval for their master was incredibly evident; they cheered as he offered them both a means for escape and a hearty dinner, which they intensely craved after months of starvation. So they came, chewing uselessly on the unforgiving concrete. Their jaws shattered intestinally, atrophying their once-membrane-surrounded organs upon contact with the stubborn concrete, which refused to budge. The weight continued to mount upon the house, but with my body safely protected under tons of solid rock, no amount of maggots could hope to penetrate.

179

Beneath the stone, I inhaled through my skin and touched my index fingers to my thumbs, meditating to the harmonies of orchestral choir music. The murmur of maggot explosions and Krüstofian screams echoed softly against the vibrating rocks. I slowly opened my eyelids with an exhale and a subtle grin.

"Showtime," I mumbled, my morning breath melting my nose-hairs.

I maneuvered my way out of the labyrinth and swiveled around my stationary feet to crack my spine. I rotated far enough around to glimpse my belly-button post-rotationally before releasing my potential energy like an elastic spring that flung back in the opposite direction, angularly oscillating until I finally spun to a stop. I proceeded to bend over backwards with an involuntary grunt, doing so violently enough that my vertebrae snapped like a celery stick and the back of my head slapped against my groin. I repeated the process in a forwards bend, catching a whiff of my kiester as I did so. Completing my morning ritual, I poked my eyes to slap some sense into the still-groggy organs. They awoke with a start to reveal an unpleasant scene:

The maggots began to crush their own brethren. They slid down the roof, frightened and urinating at the thought of almighty Death as its clammy hand gleaned their grainy souls greedily, wrenching them from their earthly bodies into the abyss of inferno. He waited for the bodies to pile and then extended a hand from the forest and pulled them underground. They molded a carcass of thousands, clumped wetly together through their own cemental secretions. Most squirmed helplessly, died voluminously, and squeaked voraciously, forgetting their physical pain and instead uselessly longing for their now-impossible dinner.

They cursed Krüstof. He had promised them a meal, but the house had held instead. They had died for him, and they had received no reward for their lacerations, while he remained unfairly unscathed. Krüstof's visage of supreme jubilee evolved grimly into pure melancholy. His plan had been foiled. He would be the laughingstock of the entire government, and they would tease him just as they always had.

"Maggot-boy!" they would say. But he was no boy; he was a man. So he ran to the maggots, scapegoating them as the culprits, assigning his failure to their blundering ineffectiveness. Standing amongst the swarm, he individually served each maggot their portion of the blame. He fumbled with his pen as he stapled culpability notices to their foreheads, reading "This is MY fault and I am an IDIOT and not Krüstof!" He despised those creatures now for tarnishing his infallible plot, a deep-seeded hatred implanted indefinitely, for now I, the bane of his existence, the droplet of nettle in his pool of calm, continued to live. The maggots were equally enraged, hating Krüstof for pressing them upon an impossible task. So the two tyrants went to war.

The battle was disgusting and pathetic. Krüstof and the maggots, two awful creations, accidental existences mistakenly overlooked by the great Beyond, clashing in the unity of antagonism, splashing in the kiddy pool of chemical insanity. One side a mass of millions of wriggling devil worms; the other an ogreish fiend trapped within the waddling body of a crab. There were still millions of surviving maggots, and Krüstof dove knee-deep into the crowd and stomped laboriously through the resulting soup, whimpering and squeaking as he over-exerted himself.

"Eh! Mmyeh! Take… that! Nyeh!" His voice steadily rose in pitch until it shattered the glass eyes of an observing nobleman, who crumpled to his knees and screamed a hard, genuine scream of Death as the shards punctured his skull.

The maggots liquified at Krüstof's piercing touch, thickening the broth in which he waded. But enough of their minuscule teeth lodged firmly into his shell, and their combined weight slowed his trek through the gook. He had been tranquilized, and he fell sloppily asleep, still gently crooning moans of frustration. Now fortune offered the maggots an opportunity to avenge the death of their brothers. Krüstof would die.

But as I watched his gross body become overtaken by the maggots, a few steamed crab legs—accompanied by lemon butter sauce and a side of creamed spinach, I imagined, salivating— already consumed, I took unexpected pity upon the man who ordered Kambu to kill my brother. He arrived here giddy with excitement, only to have his plan backfire into a murderous jamboree. I knew he hated me, but I momentarily loved him in return, and I would save him.

The maggots went easily enough. A wooden broom did the trick, bristles splintering fatally upon most maggots and sliding the rest far enough from my way to eliminate the possibility of harm. I plucked Krüstof's unconscious body from the rubble and rolled him to a maggot-free clearing. I hated myself for what I had done. I had betrayed my family. In time, I told myself, I would kill Krüstof; this I swore.

I dragged him to the village doctor's tombstone and had it care for Krüstof's wounds. He did not wake. Doctor Pons Minchus-Watlee chimed in from the heavens; he surmised it would be years, and during this time, the cabinet would wonder where its leader was. (This is not a medicine cabinet; instead, I speak of the Chancellor's cabinet of living advisors, from which he could select specific individuals for appropriate governmental situations, squeezing the men out of their tubes, sponging ideas from them, and closing the cabinet doors.) No, the truth would not suffice. I would be accused and subsequently ruled guilty of the ultimate infraction, certainly punishable by execution. I had become a fugitive once again, and it was only a matter of time before the officials would begin their hunt for me. Nowhere within the city would be safe, but I knew of one protected location. So I ran towards the forest–my place of refuge for so many years–the place of my adventures with Amadeus–to escape my transgression.

I combed through my thoughts for an idea innovative enough to scale the Great Wall, and I fingered my stringy hair in hopeful inventiveness while grinding my mental gears in thought. Few had hair as long as mine, for the corrosive chemicals in the air and moist light typically eroded exposed protein into a frizzy bundle of rot. I suddenly realized that there was only one solution.

I tore a chunk of hair from my head and held back tears. My hairs dangled in my clammy hands, gripping the contours of my callouses and infiltrating my wrinkles, entangling themselves and uprooting my fingernails. The follicles seemed to squirm supernaturally, and they exhibited a sort of sad liveliness, crying pleas for release from their bleak existence. They found comfort

183

among themselves as they fondled each other and purred like gay cuttlefish. More chunks were to come.

I merged my handfuls of hair with each other, and the chunks of my scalp glued together well enough, locking loosely. I ran out of cranial hair after only a few feet of self-produced rope, so I began to extract more from all around my body. After many tearful minutes, my rope reached a few centimeters in thickness and just sufficient length to scale the wall. I rubbed its tip upon my bleeding, bald head, and the clots stuck thickly. I swung the rope over the wall, unable to restrain a "Yeehaw," and my blood served as a perfect adhesive, permanently merging to the cement. Scaling it proved no challenge; Krüstof claimed the wall blocked the meteorological flow of clouds hundreds of miles above the planet's crust, but it was actually no more than ten feet, for Krüstof did not expect any of his subjects to dare defy his law. From the top of the wall, I swung the rope to the other side so that it would not be visible from the inside of the district but so that I could return should I need to, and I leapt into the forest.

25: A PHANTASMIC HOPE

With spicy vendetta tugging at my sleeve like a ravenous little hellion, I could not focus on my thumb war with Toakus—the forest-dwelling mushroom dwarf who I accompanied in his humble foyer. My mind drifted to fantasies of vengeance. I groped the moist shadows of my mentalz for memories of potential allies against Krüstof's regime and ideas for arms sources. Toakus' tiny, chitin-reinforced thumb firmly yet with good sportsmanship pressed mine down into our coiled fingers. The mushroom dwarf peered semi-apologetically up at me from under his biologically built-in toadstool hat, which was far wider in diameter than the dwarf's shoulders and spotted with blotches of earthy colors. The brim hung low and curled in, wilting with a dewy fungus crust that cracked in the wind and rained crumbs onto my hand. The sudden and petrifying reality of imminent defeat snapped me back into the real world. I firmly grasped Toakus' wrist with my free hand and jerked back with all my might. Toakus' shoulders dislocated as he was hurled over his sour opponent. He careened across the foyer and collided with the wall. His oh-so-fabulous chitin entirely failed to prevent his mushroom head from squashing flat on the wall like a handful of mashed potatoes thrown onto a parking garage floor, and the resounding thud was gut-wrenching. Toakus lay convulsing in a heap of fungal despair, and I spat as I marched by him, amazed at my own cruelty. I shuffled hurriedly through his front door and onto his insignificant lawn.

With four great lunging strides, I entered the thickets of the forest in which I played sword fight as a child, but the soothing

185

songs of seeds swirling in the wind to which I had grown so accustomed were drowned out by exasperated crinkling.

I peered through the wispy branches and caught sight of the spot where I had abandoned my friend Amadeus nearly two decades ago. The bag was still there, and it obviously had a noticeable opening. It still bucked and rolled, but very defeatedly. Its captive knew escape was the pipe dream of a lunatic, but punching and writhing was all he now knew. He pressed his open mouth against the wall of the bag, which crumpled inwards as he frantically inhaled.

Running towards the bag as my nostalgia panged, I failed to lift my feet sufficiently from the earth to clear a protruding root, and my ankle wedged itself between the wood and the ground. My knee retreated to the underside of my thigh and my quadriceps fell down my calves in a gravitationally-induced megacramp before I plummeted face first into the moss. As I pushed a brick of mud through my teeth with my tongue, I noticed a certain otherworldly mist swirling in wisps of blue energy around my face. I directed my gaze above me just in time to catch a glimpse of an intricately clad shaman, nostrils and eyelids flexed, as he bewitched me with a necromantic spell that granted consciousness to all of my fingers. Acting entirely independently of my control and immediately overcome with malevolent impulses, they began constricting one another to cut off circulation. They headbutted each other with fingernail helmets that sliced cleanly down to the bone.

"Oh! Please! They will kill each other!" I beseeched him. He merely observed me, judged me, scrutinized me. My fingers were all broken now, knuckles flapping in either direction as they attempted

186

in vain to continue to destroy one another. "Do not take them from me!" I cried in exasperation and despair. "They are the last things I can call mine! Oh, do not kill them in front of me!"

Finally, the godly being, teeth and bones dangling from his ornate tribal necklace, released the spell's grip upon my fingers, and they all grew limp simultaneously before slapping against the ground and spattering droplets of blood against his ancient, spectral furs.

"Kambu," he answered confidently, before I had even asked him that question.

"You… you killed my brother," I stuttered.

"Ah. Yes," he replied, his tone entirely unchanged. "For balance. And yet his demise only counteracts that of one beast. We still have work to do, boy. Murders to come."

He noticed my protesting grimace but denied me the opportunity for a retort by continuing.

"The spirits cry in agony. I feel their wails shave my veins into ribbons. They taint my cells with death and consume me with divine disease. You see, worm, order was offended. Humankind needed to play its part. And so they would burn. The scales can only tip for so long. There comes a time when the pendulum of suffering will swing through the domain of man. And when it does–" he lurked closer towards me in a cloud of murmuring darkness and nearly pressed his nose up against mine– "who will be spared?"

Allowing the aura of his final words to linger prophetically in the eerie silence of the forest, he turned away from me and retreated a few paces. I expected to hate him for my brother's murder, but I found that I could not; perhaps his incantations had

Kambu

brought about my peace, for I found him justly exempt from all established regulations of anger and emotion. His back towards me, he calmly asserted: "You seek something."

At first, I stumbled to gather my tongue and produce an intelligible response. After a brief interlude, I managed to muster a coherent sentence. "My... my friend there. In the bag. He's... stuck."

Kambu examined the imprisoned heap of limbs and organs.

"Hmm. Difficult, but not impossible. I can save him," he offered.

"Well, it looks open, actually," I observed.

"It isn't so simple, boy. You have entered the transaction. I grant your wish, and you grant mine." From the fog that purred around his ankles he swiped a handful of thick air and whirled it over his head. The circular trail he left behind used the vapor's enchanted sediment to condense into a mechanical device. "Behold: the Wheel of Consequence."

I stared at him in confusion while he waited for my response with his arms crossed; several minutes later, when I had offered him none, he threw up his hands towards the sky in frustration. Disappointed that I did not guess his intent, he cranked the lever himself, and the dreaded clicks of the spokes sang their chaotic melody in the language of the unpredictable to determine my fate. The final click revealed which punishment would be mine: "Ocular Inversion."

Kambu curled his right thumb and forefinger into a ring and pinched them around the base of his left middle finger. Squeezing tight against the bone and forcing muscles and blood vessels out of the way, the shaman swiftly rolled his two fingers up the other,

189

pushing a bulge of flesh up towards his fingertip as he did so. When the meaty bulb reached his nail, his skin ripped open and unpeeled to release the pocket's enchanted goo like a magical pimple. The blue, wet contents spewed towards me, but I sidestepped the projectile, and it splashed directly against the forehead of a small toad. The amphibian could do nothing but scream as its eyeballs rolled backwards to face the inside of its head, revealing the revolting contents of his cranium—blood vessels, tendons, skull, brain. The nerves that attached to the back of its eyes stretched to a breaking point, and one snapped in a volatile outwards pop like a severed guitar chord, leaving that eye hanging loosely in its socket only by the adhesive stick of the slimy skin that encircled it. Hopping about blindly in excruciating pain and fear, the toad smashed into a tree and slouched against the ground, still.

"Does... does that count?" I inquired hesitantly. Raising one finger to his chin, the shaman considered the plight of the natural spirits and whether his granting of my favor was requited by the death of the toad. Finally, he shrugged his shoulders.

"I suppose the energies are at harmony one way or another," Kambu declared optimistically. He meandered over to the bag and drew a white, glowing blade from thin air. Then, he proceeded to stab the bag repeatedly until the summation of each individual hole formed sufficiently large a continuous opening for the bag to tear apart like a mushroom bursting with a firm poke. Kambu turned to me and waved a casual goodbye, and as the shaman disintegrated away into the atmosphere with the biological winds, a very porous and astonished Amadeus came tumbling out.

He was appallingly malnourished and as wrinkled as a sheet of scrotum jerky left in the washer. His hairline had receded past his entire scalp and now resided inside of his body. As he wheezed feebly, the vocal distortion of his follicle-infested throat became apparent. Upon being exposed to the modest woods' sunlight, he flopped violently like a fish on the deck and howled a bloody cry. His tired bones cracked easily after years without calcium, except that of his own watery and sparse rage-induced lactations. His extra skin caught drafts and flapped wildly. The lifetime of unrelenting darkness rendered his eyes useless, and his starved body had sucked them backwards into his skull and slowly down his dry throat. They slithered loudly, and as he motioned to speak, one could see the now misshapen orbs splashing and grinding up and down his melting esophagus. The same went for his tongue, which he accidentally swallowed in his seventh year of imprisonment. At the will of Great Gorott, he had once devoured his teeth, chomping on nothing until only a finely ground enamel paste remained. He swallowed that too, and now his cavernous kisser was destitute, bereft of all dental organs. Amadeus looked a mess—a sad sight indeed.

"Oh Amadeus!" I cried, withdrawing snacks from my fanny pack. "Eat, you poor devil! It's been so long."

"Oh yes, eat I shall!" grumbled Amadeus enthusiastically, hastily accepting the food from my bloody hands. Keenly predicting that Amadeus' teeth were no more, I had brought many soft foods in my pack, including water. Amadeus wolfed them down and began to sob. He kicked the bag off, and it floated away, crackling against the Earth and pissing off nature.

191

"Sob not, my friend!" I bellowed, "The revolution is here! We're taking the old arms from the forest and fighting Krüstof!"

"Fighting? Isn't that... mean?" pondered Amadeus, the corners of his mouth flecked with sweet potato casserole.

"Well, yes, but so is Krüstof. So it's fair," I retorted, molten marshmallows gluing my teeth together and forming gooey webs as I talked.

"But... Don't you want to play bug farm?" inquired Amadeus, his lips coated in warm Greek yogurt.

"I hate the damned insect breeders!" I shouted, spraying Amadeus with a blast of refried beans. I remembered the maggot breeders who had ruined my life, and an unbridled rampage brewed within me, but Amadeus' childish, heartwarming innocence did shock me.

"Oh," mustered Amadeus as he recoiled and blinked rapidly from the bean bits. "So you never found the bag-stamper?" he casually offered, truly not intending to convey any hard feelings.

"No... Sorry." I offered modestly, my chin dripping baby food peas. Amadeus' purity and heart of gold stimulated my inner child again. I realized this was just because Amadeus had been fortunate enough to spend his whole life protected from the evils of society in his own special bag; untainted, his passion never dissolved, while mine, trapped in a prison more potent than his bag, did. Suddenly my fury made an unexpected return. "IF YOU WON'T HELP ME, I'LL GET SOMEONE ELSE!" I shrieked after stifling a gag on some canned ravioli.

"Well... Good luck!" called Amadeus cheerily, already slinking back into his bag as I stormed off with a mouthful of boiled porridge gushing out of my puss.

After the disappointing conversation with my childhood friend, I indignantly marched out of the woods with a temper hotter than a steamed vegetable. I muttered senseless profanity as feisty gnats buffeted my sweaty nape and thorny twigs nicked my nude ankles. Any fetal saplings unfortunate enough to extend their tender necks into my path were inexorably met by a fatal spinning chop. I was irate. The one-man stampede emerged from the brim of the forest seething with frustration.

"WELL THEN, WHO ELSE WILL JOIN?!" I demanded over the wall with a piercing wail that displaced fowl from their perches and silenced all nearby farmers. The only audible noise was the sound of my heavy breathing. "NO ONE?!" I exclaimed as I surveyed the adjacent countryside with a righteous optical pat down. "... Cowards." I smirked, and I was off. I knew who would help: the noblest lad I ever knew—my cousin Yuelfrik. No one had seen Yuelfrik in years after the wind took him, and I knew the task of tracking him down was in fact more than qualified to daunt. Copping a squat on a ripe and colorful toadstool in a puddle of befuddlement, I raised one finger, two eyebrows, and all of my spirits. The wind bellowed menacingly as I approached the wall. I gazed upon the bleak obstruction with pensive distaste. What now? By the Puppeteer, what NOW?

Why should I return? After all, I had no one left. Who knew where Yuelfrik was? I thought about life in the forest. I had Amadeus, and the dwarfish creatures were friendly enough. I could

193

gorge on berries, hunt freely, and escape the horrors of society. Why should I scale the wall?

I quickly found the answer. What kind of a coward would leave his people when he had a chance to bring Krüstof to justice? I could avenge my father, my brother, my kin. So I would, and I knew just how, though my solution did not include a continued search for Yuelfrik, the plan for which I had already forgotten.

I returned to Uncle Chadwick's home. His corpse welcomed me warmly with a formal salutation, and after acknowledging him briefly I ran to the medicine closet. It had been long since I had set foot here, but I remembered the exact day in detail. The jar brought back melancholy memories; I recalled vividly that I acquired the paste within in the search for cousin Yuelfrik—a search that ended in bleak failure and horrid fright as I had instead encountered the wicked home of our Chancellor. But I was undeterred.

I unscrewed the rusty lid, flecking the paint chips and dust mites away with my calloused hand. How I remembered my youth at the last time I held the jar... How long ago could it have been? My memory struggled to grasp the detail but succeeded in picturing my boyish capillaries enthusiastically pulsing oxygenous blood through my rich bones, the very bones that now reeked in decay and cracked, and the same blood that now curdled with sappy viscosity and left streaks of dark maroon on my stained skin where it escaped the confinements of my damaged veins. I couldn't help but think I no longer had capillaries; no structure that fine could persist in a body as ravaged as my own. Nor did I believe in my veins, for my extremities were in such constant pain that I was convinced the blood merely flowed freely within my skin like water in a plastic bag, my bones floating aimlessly throughout like scattered twigs, eroding and dampening in the fluid until their eventual complete decomposition.

I soggily gripped the jar with my balloonish fingers, and my index reached in to scrape up the still fresh-maggogoo. Happily did I smear it again upon my cheek. Happily was it met by my choking skin whose pores had been clogged by ash and soot, now absorbed by the moisture of the solution. Conniving was my smile as I looked into the mirror, for I knew that a spring lay compressed at my fingertips, and at my trigger it would release. Staring at my uncle's storytelling lips, his fibbing tongue that had recanted the tales of the villagers, I thanked him for his lies. Though I may have thought them a fictional ploy to pass the dreadful hours in Grunty Kraba, I now saw them for what they truly were: essential uniting elements of an otherwise entirely fragmented society. Should these tales plant a seed of truth, perhaps the people would invest themselves in the seed's development into a mighty oak. Perhaps Larwa Chłopak could not galvanize the revolution, but the legendary Ghost Boy certainly could. Unlike all other revolutionary attempts, this one could not die, for it was an idea—an eternal creature that could thrive as long as there remained ears through which to be heard and minds through which to be interpreted. It would outlive the body of a man, and no bullet would be powerful enough to quench its revolutionary thirst. My thoughts ran wild as I contemplated the possibility that this myth could lead our resistance to victory.

Why be a mere mortal—one who succumbs to the pull of a trigger or the swing of a blade? Why waste essence in a body so easily forgotten, decomposed and rid of, recycled into the Earth like so many millions of others—another grain in a sea of homogenous sand? Why be a man, when I could be a legend? Get off the toilet, Earth. Adventure calls.

26: A CRANE DELIVERS A FRANKENCOUP

The villagers stirred, mouths agape and drule manifesting. They had never seen a man like the one that stood before them, his words clouded by their confusion. He seemed to mutter something about ribosomes… no. Re-bunions perhaps? It didn't matter. What mattered to them was his astonishing appearance. His brash cheeks and pleading eyes seemed youthful and boyish, and the once-hopeless workers took pity on his still hopeful self, for they remembered what it had been to believe the world yet had love to offer them. The boy's skin was pale white, glowing with excited radiance, and he seemed to flow as he ran, gliding gracefully among the highest-soaring eagles, yet never leaving the ground. It did not take much to convince onlookers that I was the Ghost Boy of their legends. They had always dreamt of him—a being they desired enough to convince themselves of the legend's validity. They had long sought an excuse to rebel, but without this driving impetus they had exhibited neither the necessary courage nor the organization. They finally ceased their mindless gazes and replaced them with intently focused ears. No, he had not been chanting Rob Ellen, they thought. He said rebellion.

We began to practice in organized union for the war. We knew there would be resistance, and we would be greatly outnumbered. We had few weapons to wield, other than the metal swords and hammers Amadeus and I had forged in our youth in the forest, which were crude and dull, and which were only numerous enough to equip ten of our warriors, leaving the hundreds of others entirely unarmed. We had no experience in war, for no war had been fought in Grunty Kraba since the territory was taken over an

197

unknown number of years ago in what had been a hilariously easy enterprise met with almost no resistance at all.

Although I was their general, I had nearly nothing to offer my warriors. I was disgusting and feeble, and I had never fought before. I attempted meager training sessions with no success, for the only incompetence greater than my coaching was the performance of my subjects. They seemed incapable of concentrating for more than a few seconds, and would often doze off or chase nearby gnats. My less-than-captivating lessons droned on without response.

"Go like THIS," I hopelessly uttered while flicking my wrist in a circular pattern, "to block stuff." My stutters and gurgles were met by unimpressed stares. "Jump around... and... kill the bad men... with your fists. Ok?" Silence.

Boiling in my frustration, I was unpleasantly surprised by two immense fingers pinching my puny head and lifting me into the sky. My skin flapped and tore against the wind as I rocketed through the stratosphere before finally resting on the stomach of the culprit I had long since identified. There, on the second floor of the Earth, floated Tarfüglio in a typical state of uncontrollable amusement, and though I typically enjoyed his company, his untimely intrusion succeeded only in furthering my anxiety. I did not have time for his games.

"Tarf, can't we talk later? I'm trying to train an army, and–"

"YAOU! YAOU WHAT?" His face elongated in genuine amazement, and he poked his head out from his shoulders as he spoke, his lips rounded and his eyes squished entirely out from their sockets. "YAOU SAEY... YAOU... AAAHUEEHAEH! THE PYUNY CRAB MAEN! HE... HE... AAAAAAAHHHHH!"

"Shhh! Tarfüglio, keep it down! What if he hears you?" His gums vented a burning plasma as he relaxed his facial muscles. "Now I'm serious. I have to get to work!"

Mildly disappointed, he gradually slowed his seismic breathing. Somewhere on the ground, a man who had invested a fortune into reinventing the wind turbine had his proposal rejected when all wind abruptly halted and the energy source was deemed unreliable as subject to the whims of an over-expressive giant.

But after a brief moment, he remembered what I had said, and it excited him more than he had discipline to contain.

"Aeehueeheh… Remoember whaet yaou sed? AAAAAHOOEE! ABOEUT THE STEUPID MAEN! AND HE WAES MED AT YAOU!"

"He doesn't know. He's not—"

Now his voice exceeded the constraints of the space-time continuum. Existence warped, and time fissures rippled from his agape mouth. He immediately and sloppily plugged his still seething vocal cords, but the damage had been done: Krüstof had heard, and for the first time in his life, he tilted his neck so as to look upon the skies. What he saw terrified him; the biocity posed a direct threat to his undisputed authority. He jumped the hundreds of miles between our world and theirs, mentally lassoed the beings, and selected the "delete" option on his torso-mounted settings panel.

"So this is where you were. Nice try, boy," Krüstof chuckled smugly. The beautiful giant world began to disintegrate before my daunted eyes. I steamed in futile exasperation, royally angered that I could do naught but watch as the friendly Biglands fell to pieces as

199

soon as governmental jurisdiction interfered with their peaceful existence.

"Gao foer yaou, Lorwa. I will staey," Tarfüglio calmly uttered, what seemed to me strangely out of character. I knew he had accepted death, and he flickered holographically, hovering the void between this life and the next. I reluctantly stepped off the world and gradually floated to safety miles below, and the soft moans of a hurting Tarfüglio rang behind me. I could hear that obnoxious crabman rejoicing in beating the pacifist beasts above me with his bear claws, and they sobbed submissively, never attempting to sink to his earthly moral level with a returned blow.

Tarfüglio's already ravaged eyes leaked empty for the last time. He smiled meekly, crying, or sweating, or melting, bidding his beloved "Lorwa" goodbye. His meat stripped apart, choice cuts falling to the thankful earth, and the village feasted victoriously that night, as did Krüstof, though the crabman did greedily hoard all meat upon which he happened, screaming at any commoners who dared nibble at "his" dinner. But I only feasted on my solid tears—those that rolled lazily into my open, wailing mouth. Training would resume only once I could contain my sorrow.

27: Exposure of Sog

Gone. Astonishing. All gone. Such an untamed, unrestricted nature, destroyed by one mere man. And he was only one, I thought, in a sea of thousands more like him, willing to die to protect their leader. How were we to win? We all believed the government's forces were impeccably trained and brutally unforgiving, though there had never surfaced any propaganda regarding the military. Our beliefs came solely from our logic; the assumption that an oppressive tyrannical government would bear the most fearsome of armies was reasonable. This, of course, we did not take as an estimation, but as a fact: Krüstof certainly led a terribly skilled army.

But as training progressed I identified our crucial advantage above the overlords: we had something for which to fight. I observed the men I led, the grief in their eyes, the overwhelming desire to prove themselves adequate, to prove themselves men, to protect their sons, to preserve the force of humanity. We fought for our families, for their deaths, for the restoration of our quality of life. They fought merely because they had to.

Onwards we marched.

We courageously approached Krüstof's looming home. Its shadow crept upon our unshaken faces, poking and stinging us like a pestering tokoloshe, but its efforts to deter us were met with the stoic physiognomies of rebellious champions. His silhouette fluttered through the windshield, frantically dashing to and fro, hinting to us that he was incredibly flustered at the lack of security that allowed armed forces to march unopposed up to his creaky front porch, which, if alive, would have complained of severe epidermal aching as hundreds of bony feet scraped splinters off its abdomen. I

201

massaged my diaphragm as I prepared to summon Father C24's murderer.

"Krüstof! Get your naughty tushie out here!" I choked quaveringly. The same glass-eyed man who had observed Krüstof's attack on my mansion and who had since repaired his ocular orbs once again doubled over in agony as my high-pitched squeal shattered his eyes and penetrated his skin. He screamed and lamented his poor positioning, vowing to live underground from then on to avoid more optical devastation.

I suddenly realized the stupidity of our actions. Surely we would all die at the hands of our oppressors, for the little training my army was focused enough to understand had been mediocre at best. I had no experience and no credentials to lead an army. The face paint that branded me as Ghost Boy mocked me, for I knew I could never achieve his infinite power, and wearing his color ashamed me as I realized I could only label myself a mere wannabe who disgraced the name of a dignified figure. What kind of legend couldn't teach his army to fight? I realized that assuming the role of the Ghost Boy was a selfish, desperate attempt to push the revolution, for I felt oppressed and, thinking only of my burning thirst to avenge my family, convinced myself to put the lives of our entire village at risk for immediate governmental overthrow. But a revolution of what and why I did not really understand. What did I expect to change if Krüstof died? Would he not be merely replaced by a ruler of superior evil—one who would exhibit even stricter regulations in precaution that the sector would not once again be overtaken by its citizens? I knew the revolution was necessary, and once there existed enough security to back up its survival after a successful coup, along with a unified, humanistic zeitgeist, no force would be able to halt it; of this I was certain. Far too many of my loved ones died advocating the revolution, and I had felt burdened to fight as well, so I had created a rushed, sloppy effort to light the revolutionary flame.

Moreover, did the revolutionaries truly believe my hastily thrown together ghost disguise? It was infantile; all of the members of our village knew my face well, and the addition of the maggo-paste wouldn't be enough to mask my identity. I had known it all along, yet I had convinced myself that my army believed my lie. They only indulged me, pretending to believe me, as if I were a child. For whom, then, if my followers knew me Larwa, did I pretend to be Ghost Boy? Was it a ploy to scare Krüstof—to convince him that I was a man? But this would not impress him. I didn't understand what Krüstof had seen and the gorey truths he had come to accept. A Ghost Boy would not scare him.

So for what was I risking the lives of all Grunty Kraba's inhabitants? I had no confidence, no experience, and no plan. My heartstrings tremored in tampered agony, for I felt ashamed that I risked my people's lives for my personal desires.

But I had little time for my shame to culminate into retreat, for it was then that the forest's surface rumbled. I stared at the sheet of trees, a towering wall of greenery that straddled the horizon like a stair-step from the earth into the heavens, as its seemingly infallible impenetrability ruptured. Ah, the elegance of the forest! So did it contrast the bleak gloom of Grunty Kraba, its natural majesty a perfect opposite to the man-made dysphoria of the village. So did it resonate with the sounds of life, the echoes of the teeming ecosystem that within it thrived. So did it exemplify the model of society that humans had intended to replicate, providing clear evidence that our attempt at creating a blossoming environment in what we called "civilization" was a ridiculous failure. For while the forest bloomed–screamed in the vigor of survival, surged with the power of existence–our pathetic attempt at a dynamic between the untamed enterprise of natural biology and the rigid structure of obnoxious societal order proved an utter fiasco. Our society crumbled, our people died, and, worst of all, their deaths came as a sweet release to the bleak alternative of life. But I digress.

Millions of tiny bodies marched through the thickets. Their asymmetrical mutations tainted the poetically beautiful landscape. Their cries of war bellowed louder and louder as the comical army approached and prepared to merge with ours, equally uproarious in our mediocre skill. Two of them stepped into the eye sockets of the glass-eyed man, who had dug a hole in the dirt in which he had planned to lie forever, but who now sprinted into the forest, crying and cursing. Some hobbled, some flew, some rolled; but no matter the means of transportation nor the drastic physical differences between them all, they remained united under a strange sense of speciesism. Comparing them to our army, though our soldiers towered at ten times their height, I knew they boasted more strength, for one goal united them: the repayment of a debt to their savior. The Żuk had come.

They saluted as they had that day so many years ago. They were armed with various whips and knives forged with artisanal perfection from wood or earth metals, and they were meticulously trained in the art of war. As they met my startled gaze, they silently swore to obey my every command, and I knew their disciplined battle abilities (for they were well known for their organized war tournaments between adults, required weekly from the age of two months until death ten years later) would come in handy when waging war against the government's tenacious military. Suddenly, gauging our newfound army, I reasoned that we stood a chance. The Żuk may have been small, but they had collective immensity on their side—in numbers as well as uniformity of mind—and their skill proved tremendous in battle. Our human army may have been unskilled, but unity sprouted from our hatred of the government we sought to overthrow; our fight would be spirited and passionate.

And looking around, I realized my efforts wouldn't be wasted. Krüstof was as mortal as any other, and enough rebellious spirit would topple his rule. The entire colony lived under meager oppression. Food was scarce, water was polluted, health was undermined. The villagers had no idea how horrible their suffering truly was, for this abhorrent nature couldn't be compared to any past experiences. They had no reference point—no other, stable society to which they could compare their dystopian one; at no point had they tasted the nectar of freedom. None should be forced to live under the abominable Gruntian conditions.

Future Larwa popped out from my pocket and slapped me silly. I realized that, regardless of whether the rebellion was inspired by my selfish spite towards Krüstof, it would ultimately benefit the people.

I cleared my mucky throat, poisoned by the thick musk of the wet air, and tried again. "KRÜSTOF, YOU PATHETIC MAGGOT-BOY!" The insult slid off my tongue like a baby off an icy driveway. I had never heard the phrase uttered in my life, but somehow I knew it fit. Instantaneously, his figuratively authoritative man-hat turned backwards with a single roll of the tongue, demoting him from big man of Grunty Kraba to a mere chibby-chub boy, eating wing-things and dancing in public, drowning in shame. He roared ferociously within his chambers, stammering to retort cleverly, but producing an embryo of a comeback: he managed only a few unintelligible mutters as he clumsily slid on his slippers to confront our masses face to face.

"But... you are not... popular? And... you are fat," the supreme obese-lord mumbled. The tiny man driving his emotions rerouted his confusion into the anger outlet. "You think you'll get away with this? I'll kill you, transgressor! I'll have you fed to the maggots! YOU CAN'T DO THIS TO ME! YOU MUST NOT KNOW ME, BOY!" he squawked back, seething with the divine rage characteristic only of the sector's most temperamental ever Chancellor.

"Oh, I know who you are. You're the Maggot-Boy who killed my family. Maggot-Boy." I grunted. The snarky comment fueled my ego. "We're here to kill you. And you can't do anything about it. What are you gonna do, pinch our butts, Crab Man?"

Krüstof struggled to comprehend this disobedience. None had ever dare question his authority. None, of course, but two. What had that man's name been? And the boy? He remembered the faces now, and one word came to mind: Smutny. Then another: Ślimak. Of course, he thought. Now it all made sense! The evil child before him was Smutny's son, Ślimak's brother, and his presence owed itself to vengeance. That fart so many years ago... it had been

206

his! What a poor, misled idiot. After all, his fatherly figure and stupidly dead brother were nothing but wretched transgressors. No wonder he had grown up such a spoiled brat.

"You must be confused. Do not worry. You did not say those words. Your Mag-O-Gag stopped that. What you actually told me was 'I am poop and you are pretty. I yield to your crabby omniscience. Heil Krüstof.'" The crab-legged meatman concluded his point with triumphant pride. I stared him in the face, unmoved and silent, my hollow cheeks coating the gag like an elastic sock. I seemed older now, and much more mature. I could feel my eye bags drooping and shaking as I moved like inversed pockets filled with cottage cheese. My stomach perpetually bellowed with the heavy, clunkish feeling of liquid filling, though I was always inexplicably thirsty, and the moist air condensed into beads of desert-dry sweat upon my skin, leaching out the ammonia and dripping poisonously onto the infertile earth, seeping through the cracks and into the toxic sea.

He was right, I knew. The Mag-O-Gag had kept me human. None had ever known its true purpose until now: it had been designed to suppress anti-government speech, but it had never been activated in anyone, for no one had ever boasted the intellectual capacity to question the system. Listening intently, I could hear the muffled bubbles I had once perceived as language. All this time my subjects had learned nothing because my ideas had been replaced by ordinary conversation through the artificially intelligent Mag-O-Gag.

EXAMPLE: a simple command such as "Shoot!" would change to "I like sadness."

207

My plans and conspiracies had never been truly understood. Only in the forest with Amadeus, where the signal of the gags would cut off due to distance, were my thoughts truly conveyed. I had been duped.

"Everything I've ever said has been pointless. Nice." I mocked myself and laughed at my ignorance, offended by my mean comments. I wondered if anything anyone had ever said to me had been at all valid.

I reached into my throat and clasped the gag timidly, my fingers struggling to firmly grip the squeaky, wet surface. Krüstof smirked happily. I reached in further, finally clenching the metallic cord that seemed to descend into my esophagus. The pain sharply pulsated through my spine and burned ferociously, but my determination had become clear, and Krüstof had taken notice.

"Hey, stop… Stop that! What are you doing? STOP!" He struggled to control the situation as the crowd began gasping at the unthinkable act. I began tugging the cord from my throat, but it was deeply rooted, and I could feel it wrenching my ribcage up as I attempted to remove it. But my ribs were small and weak anyways, and, I thought, I could always grow a new set. With one gargantuan tug I severed the attachment of my ribcage to my pelvis, launching bone splinters throughout my already feeble bloodstream. Gag, cord, various teeth, and bones alike spattered from my mouth in a bloody heap, dripping spinal fluid and battery acid. The people in the crowd, along with a wildly enraged Krüstof, were flabbergasted.

"I–" like a newborn fawn stumbling in its first steps, my shaky voice struggled to control itself, for I had never been able to successfully criticize the government with the gag still in my mouth–

"I... hate.... THE GOVERNMENT!" I finally screamed. Krüstof messily wept and nearly fainted with astonishment while six servants dabbed at his tears with fur handkerchiefs. None had more severely offended him than I. I continued: "You crabby Maggot-Boy. You were right. I have the fire. And you will burn along with oppression. Grunty Kraba will be saved!" I daringly proclaimed. The crowd broke into wild cheering as they even further consecrated my greatness as their legendary Ghost Boy leader.

"Fidel! Fidel! Fidel!" The praises emulated from their lips, and the surge of enthusiasm boosted my confidence immensely, though my stomach whimpered sorrowfully from its nearly fatal injury. "Look at us! We are no longer an unheard voice; you will listen to the flames licking your chops. I challenge your royal military to defeat the army that stands before it!" I caustically demanded.

I expected a clever retort or a willful demonstration of government dominance but was instead met with the flustered stutters of a man unmasked. "Um... We will fight, and... win.. yes, you morons! We have... a large... military..." stammered a confused Krüstof. He seemed to forget language for momentary lapses, then yelling any words that suddenly came to him. "And! ... Besides!... TODAY!"

The illusion of the governmental military, I realized, had been lifted. Krüstof had counted on the assumption that no organized rebellion would ever solidify, for, he believed, the villagers lived under too much fear to dare to fight. They had no authority figure educated enough to cause uproar within the illiterate masses; education was largely stumped for this very purpose. And he had been correct in all assumptions but one, for the authority figure did in fact emerge, and his name was Ghost Boy. Saltwater tears in which swam giant Egyptian crocodiles silently dripped down the weakened overlord's cheeks, and the audience members' mouths gaped in disbelief. Their once-almighty leader had broken down into infantile sobs. He had no military, and ours, although no match for a full scale army, presented a formidable threat against him alone. He, it seemed, was grossly underprepared for our uprising, and Żuk and human alike wailed in furious fervor, anxious to begin the rebellion that had existed in a dormant state for so many years, long overdue for awakening. We charged the doorway, and the battle had begun.

28: A Curious Inferno

I screamed in savagery, and my mouth foamed at the thought of getting my hands on some Krüstof crab-cakes. Strangely, however, I couldn't remember why. I wasn't exactly certain what Krüstof had actually done to me to merit this rebellion, but I did remember that he deserved whatever was to come. I looked at my fellow companions, and I realized I could no longer tell the difference between the human soldiers and the Żuk. I leered at the sky, but it was not the sort of vast window into oblivion that most skies were. Instead, this sky was confined, pressed up against some kind of force field, against something I could not see. But somehow I knew that the sky was contained and finite, and the thought made me shudder. My vision seemed blurred; what appeared to be heat waves rose from my eyelids and distorted everything I saw. More importantly, fury and cannibalistic rage blinded my aching eyes, and only my bloodlust for Krüstof caught the focus of my fleeting mind.

My peepers—my poor, abused peepers, bleeding from all they had seen, weeping from all they had not—darted frightenedly to and fro, for it seemed to me that my companions were undergoing metamorphosis. Their muscles bulged veinily, and hairs sprouted from their rippling skin. Their teeth elongated into serrated fangs; their nails into ferocious claws. And most disturbing of all, their arms began to run alongside their legs, and their bipedalism was lost in evolutionary oblivion. But the moon was new, I considered; superstition justified not these unsettling howls...

Was my skin changing color?

211

Our cries lacerated the sound barrier and came as a lucid awakening to an aghast Krüstof, who only now took seriously the rebellion that he had previously so underestimated. The abrupt realization that his power faced serious threat for the first time since my brother's attempted murder twelve long years ago piqued his anxious mind. He sobbed fetally; mucus bubbles inflated at his nostrils and evaporated into the already thick air as their surfaces became exposed to the sweltry heat, further curdling the atmosphere. He bolted at maximum overdrive–a skimpy 5 kilometers per hour–from the amassing horde of revolutionaries, but the mob continued to encroach upon the division between them and their oppressor. His time was near.

I reached out to a silhouette of his body and snatched at the air, but when I pulled away, I found that my hand had only grasped a drooping fluid of rainbow hue. I jumped as high as possible, but in the air I realized this was pointless. Despite my desperate downwards thrusts, I seemed unable to return to the ground, and I believe I reached four thousand feet. But this is ridiculous, so it was probably more like two or three. I didn't care, and I continued to chase him from the clouds.

The time came when I began to waft his nautical stench, and my hand stretched to mere inches away from his thinning hairline. If only I could make one final surge, I thought, I could take hold of those wisps of silvery twine and yank Krüstof to the ground. I revolved my legs at turbo-speed, but they moved too quickly to gain traction with the ground, so I remained stationary as my frictionless feet swiftly swept the earth's slippery surface. I tripped over my shoelaces, but I had no shoes, so I did not fall until I had already

212

reached the ground, and I scrunched my face in preparation for collision with the coarse earth. But I never met the dirt, for when my body was parallel to the floor, the soil opened up into a new, vertical world perpendicular to ours into which I could safely continue running downwards. A man was running away from me in the distance, and I assumed it was Krüstof. I had lost ground, I disappointedly thought, so I toggled some settings and was soon off in DOUBLE MEGA BOOST MODE. But no matter how much I increased in speed, the figure before me kept its distance. Krüstof suddenly ran directly across my path, heading due west to my north, cackling in temporary triumph. I stared at him, confused, and looked back at the figure who had been running from me. He stared back at me and waved politely. It was me, but I seemed much younger. A mirror stood before me, I hesitantly reasoned, unconvinced.

My distemper boiled, for I would not be humiliated by an old geezer. I wanted to kill Krüstof more than ever. I yearned to strangle him—to choke his windpipe until his eyes popped and his veins leaked clotted blood—until his lips turned black and his skin crackled like the salty sands of a severely dehydrated desert and brittlely broke away from his bony muscles and muscular bones. I salivated at the thought of eating his fishy flesh. I wanted to kill that fiend, to desecrate his corpse, to feed him to his own maggots. I sought blood, and the once blurry line was no more. What was humane?

Krüstof had slowed. He seemed to hug a large, obese tree, one that rose perpendicularly with respect to the earth and towered in symmetry, cut off flatly at the top and sparsely populated by vines or branches. I sneered in jubilance, for apparently I would now be able to capture his crabby ass. I blinked, but when my eyes

213

reopened there was no Krüstof, and in his place squirmed a krakomaggot.

"BLUAGH!" it snarled. I recoiled in fear as its outstretched tentacles puckered wetly upon my skin, but after one more blink the beast was no more. Krüstof stood there once again, but organic matter no longer composed the object he held. Instead: metal, and that of a familiar breed—the maggot silo. And Krüstof lifted it from its roots in the ground with ease, snapping pipes and demolishing the foundation as he did.

I screamed at my army to retreat; they did not listen. I warned them of what was to come; their beastly ears would have none of it. I wondered if they were too uncivilized to understand; they replied with guttural, inscrutable grunts bellowing from deep within their esophageal tracts. They seemed unable to use their tongues for speech, for they had forgotten how to maneuver them. They had come to fight, and fight they would, but the battle before them could not be won. Krüstof flung the silo.

Had the confrontation taken place four or five years earlier, perhaps the maggot silo would not have been an impossible obstacle. But the once-space-shuttle had been modified to house millions more maggots than before, with two new storage chambers attached to each side. Radioactive waste (I always theorized that this was merely Krüstof's excrement) constantly poured into the silo, and this combined with Krüstof's growing interest in genetically altering his maggots bred a fearsome plethora of new-and-improved maggot warriors. The species could never be fully documented, for within each there existed many subspecies along with a handful that seemed not to fit into any classification at all, until, of course, one realized that they could create a new species altogether, though even this somehow seemed illogical. Names have only been adopted for the most prominent species; I list those whose names are concise enough to transcribe:

"Classic" Maggots: maggot; maggocattle; scavenger maggot.

Upgraded: frankenmaggot; maggohound; serpomaggot; crocomaggot; rhinomaggot; arachnomaggot; scorpomaggot; polymaggot; maggonoid; reaper-maggot…

ULTRA Upgraded: dracomaggot; galactomaggot; tyrannomaggot; krakomaggot; gigamaggot; cybermaggot; solar-maggot; sasquatchomaggot; maggolythic-golem; ectomaggot; carbomaggot…

They came too quickly, lunging upon us before we had a chance to react. The initial impact of the silo, weighing millions of tons, crushed an unfathomable number of our men—too high to be quantified by mortal numbers. I barrel-rolled from its path, barely inching out of the fatal cemetery that the silo instantly established upon its landing on the thenfound site of countless rebel graves. I sobbed, but I had warned them. Their own stupidity, I thought, had brought about their deaths, for they should not have defied the will of their commander. It would be up to me, then, and my few remaining soldiers, to defeat Krüstof.

All remaining warriors trudged knee-deep through maggot jelly. The worms gnawed at our calves and eventually our bones, picking away ligaments and releasing blood and veins into the maggoty mix. Walking became nearly impossible, and only a few steps at a time could be taken before one lost his breath and was

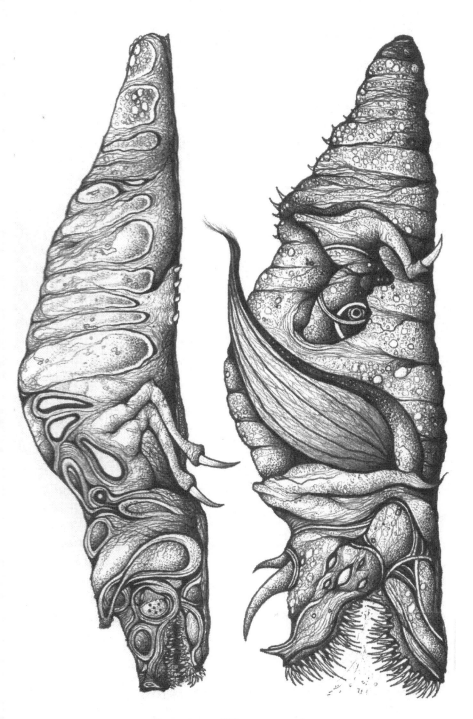

Maggohound/Dracomaggot

forced to take a break to look for it. Krüstof smiled, pulled out his reading glasses, paper and pen, and began to sketch, levitating a few inches above the maggot pool, glowing with the angelic enlightenment of infinite knowledge. I plowed through the maggots, slowly edging closer to him. I was enraged by his arrogance; as I sought to murder him, he had the audacity to nonchalantly doodle and enjoy the hot tub/simmering cesspool above which he floated. I approached him, bereft of any plan, but certain that I would emerge triumphant.

Suddenly, Krüstof's sullen expression transformed into an ear-to-ear grin. His eyes widened, and his dry lips cracked and bled as they stretched into his menacing sneer. He revealed his drawing to me, depicting a victorious tyrant–certainly the crabbo himself–rectifying himself with a conquering stamp of his foot upon the mound of defeated common men.

I could not accept this alternate scenario in which I lost this battle. I was so fixated upon my permanence in this world that my immortality had been certain until I saw Krüstof's wish fulfillment of my death. Incomprehension stimulated my rage. I screamed once again, but this time I could not stop. My lungs uncorked, and until all my air had been expelled, my incessant wailing would not cease. Unbeknownst to me, since my anger had taken control of my bones and relieved my brain of its processing duties, my fist plunged into Krüstof's crunchy face. Blood spattered into the air and coated my already greasy hair, and Krüstof shot backwards at a ridiculously high speed, backflipping through the air at millions of miles per hour, 40,000 feet above sea-level (unfortuitously, this measurement may have been false, for rumors suggested that Grunty Kraba was

Over The Common Man

submerged in the Pacific). Simultaneously with my omega-argon-punch, the entire world combusted into a massive conflagration as Krüstof's meteoric form whizzed past, and the fiery winds flared with such power that they reverted Mother Earth into paralysis. But the fire of revolution, I reasoned, had long before begun.

Krüstof instantly recovered from the strike, set aside the mirror he had been holding–or had that been a drawing?–and loaded his 1570 X-model Luger. He never expected anyone to survive his first shot, which, he assumed, was impeccably accurate and more powerful than any shot fired by another man with the same arm.

I did not hear the gunshot fire. I did not feel the bullet pierce my stomach. Nor did I notice the ambient explosions, or the tyrannomaggot swallow the patriot to my left, or the death of three others at the hands of a maggot feeding frenzy. A long-chinned man screamed something at me, but the sounds were vague and blurry.

"Why are your eyes small? Your cheeks are large. Your eyes look squished," I did not say. He was screaming something…

"You've been shot!" he squealed, but I did not understand. "You're bleeding! You must go to the hospital!" I averted the statements; the three-dimensional words projected towards my ears, but I performed a sweet spin move to dodge their impact. Instead of hearing, I focused on the fact that the man was not helping our rebellion.

"You do not fight for the rebels?" I inquired accusingly.

"Larwa, I told you. I do not want to hurt anyone!" he replied.

"Erm… If you do not fight for us, then you fight against us!" I reasoned uncertainly. I drew a grand saber from the sheath of a

219

corpse's flesh, and I swung it at the man's oversized chin. It sliced cleanly through his tender meat (his bones were unusually young and underdeveloped, as if underexposed to solar vitamins), and his once-prominent chin fell limply to the floor. He screamed in agony, but he could no longer speak decipherably. He babbled and wept, and his pleading eyes asked me the humbling question: why?

I did not care. He was a traitor, I thought. He did not deserve to speak if those words would not condemn the government as an institution deserving annihilation. He held his bleeding chin in his hands, fondly remembering the days of full-chinitude that had blessed his childhood, tears slowly creeping down his supple skin. Perhaps he said that he had found a discarded drawing of me, but that was of Krüstof, I knew... It was of Krüstof!

I remembered what he had told me about the bullet that had allegedly pierced my stomach. Fortunately, time had been moving especially slowly, so the lead slug had only moved inches from the exit wound. I thought for a moment about the man, and after some brief consideration, I decided that I remembered him granting me chronomagical powers, for, I recalled, he was the most powerful *wizard on the planet. I then signed the ancient hand signal to initiate paramount revochronation—the most superior form of desequencing practiced in all martial arts. I flipped the signal back the way it came, and the pesky cartridge promptly backtracked through my spine, sealing the skin and chiropractically adjusting my splinters back into a healthy backbone. I felt my heart and lungs shift back into their canonical locations. The bullet sailed resolutely out my chest, erasing the carnal blemish and rocketing into my shooter, Krüstof. Luckily for the arthropodal monarch, a lazy, half-hearted rebel resided within his arm's reach. The man wandered around aimlessly, discontent with his social and economic situation yet unwilling to apply the necessary effort to better his conditions, for he stood only a few feet from Krüstof and could easily have attacked and wounded the dictator with even minimal effort. This unfortunate lowlife found himself in the wrong place at the wrong time as he fell victim to Krüstof's grip and was thrust into the path of the returning bullet, which punctured his weak, spineless body with laughable ease. The grievous affliction exceeded the degenerate's mortiferal tolerance and laid him with the corn. May you serve your rapacious nation in death as well, as auxiliary to this fruitful crop or fodder for the mæg.

> *The luxury of boasting the title of "The Most Powerful Wizard on The Planet" previously belonged to Dreledon - Dreledon the Dinklehead that is. Now that may sound a wee bit harsh, but let me explain to you ol' Drelly-don as we know him here in Grunty Kraba. Dreledon's first card trick was performed at age four: making water come out of his mouth. His childhood was broadcasted in the public theatres, and the citizens of Grunty Kraba empathized with the growing wizard star as he rose to fame in his career. Men often ate their shirts in celebration of Dreledon's trademark card illusion: spontaneously generating a circle onto the card from thin air. This is highly impressive. Drelly's popularity continued to soar as his shows became ever more expensive, often demanding adults pay entry with their own fingers or their children. Before Krüstof came to power, Chancellor Olaf granted Dreledon the key to every door in the sector, along with the largest and most magically powerful wizard hat.*

Dreledon sported the brainwashing hat for all his performances thenceforth, for it granted him mind control powers that always enthralled the crowd; no spectator of Dreledon's wizardry could hope to endure an entire performance without smiling uncontrollably and wetting themselves in absolute delight. The wizard rode the tidal wave of his popularity across decades, always dazzling audiences with his same circle trick. But when Krüstof took control of the sector, he performed a flawless block on the magic ray and remained unimpressed with the magician. During one of Dreledon's famed shows, the wizard attempted to pull a card from a top-hat, but instead found within his fingers a handful of hair. He pulled from the depths of the hat the head of Krüstof himself, and he tossed the Chancellor on the floor, wiping his hand against his robe and cringing in disgust. Proudly declaring that all phony wizards would have their wizard hats shrunk by federal decree, Krüstof aimed a remote control at Dreledon's hat and selected "Zoom Out," and the hat shriveled upon the sniffling magician's scalp. The crowd stared in shock at the five-centimeter tall embarrassment atop Dreledon's head, and they began to mumble in amazement, gradually beginning to notice how childish and underwhelming the wizard's act had truly always been. They threw stones at the weeping wizard, and he tripped on his robe as he attempted to flee. As a final insult, Krüstof sentenced Dreledon to three years attempting to bury his shame in the dirt using only a toothbrush as a shovel.*

I shot an unforgiving glance at that chinless man who seemed to consider himself my self-appointed moral coach, and as his eyes met mine, they portrayed utter shock and confusion. My vision distorted dreadfully, and for a moment I considered changing the diaper that I was convinced he glamorously bore. But my seelookers cleared, and my vision failed to believe their input, for the data collected was inhumane and atrocious. His absent chin gaped and gushed gallons of thinning blood; after a few minutes the leaking liquid exhibited a milky-pink hue. Mirroring his tears, mine streamed warmly off my eyelashes (but failed to roll further than my cheekbones on account of my skin's dehydration and resulting absorption of any moisture it contacted). I realized the man whose mutilation my uncivilized acrimony produced was none other than my beloved Amadeus.

29: WHEN THE DEITIES TREMBLE

Amid the carnage, two men, one royalist and one rebel, both defraternitized by war, but united again by war alike, sparred at the highest level of martial eloquence, gracefully lunging and swooping like well-rehearsed dance partners. They used only their teeth–their deadliest and most immediate weapons. Short range yet extremely wieldable and sharp, the canines were the obvious utensil of preference; they curled back their lips and snarled with the most refined savagery, for though they had forgotten their humanness, this was a gentlemen's duel indeed. Arms back and necks extended to an inhuman degree, the selfless gallants demonstrated the utmost arête, complimenting each other's parries and nodding approvingly upon their more skillful attempts. Finally, their two teeth clashed in a brief collision of mortal determination. The royalist's tooth proved stronger, and the rebel's chipped off; the perilous predicament appeared to be his end, but the desperate bugger employed one unforeseen cheapshot of the boot. This brutish and dirty attack was a misdemeanor compared to the fatal tooth slashes exhibited before, but it did stun the royalist long enough for his carotid artery to be sufficiently drained. He fell back, hat in hand, after a reluctant salute to his competitor, and landed lightly, dry as a dogfish's deathbed. I commended the victor and do not waver in my judgement to this day.

Another pair looked deeply into each other's eyes, which only offered lifeless, unsympathetic, unwavering war gazes. Each combatant saw his own reflection in the dark, killing pupils in still scenes from various dimensions. The royalist saw himself reflected in a blooming sunbathed garden of dandelions and cattails painted in the style of impressionism. The rebel saw the image of his situation as a projection from a nineteenth century movie reel depicting the engagement as a Wild West shootout, complete with ten gallon hats and nubuck vests with tassels for all present. The reflections within reflections continued indefinitely, thrusting the duelers through well-known as well as raw, untamed dimensions. They finally synchronized planes in a digital format. Each rode advanced interboards–holographic surfboards cyberkinetically capable of zooming through 2-D terrains at the speed of information. Their reflective jogger cybersuits clung tenaciously to their calves and forearms, but flapped through the algebraic winds of the coordinate universe. They wielded deadly baton staffs with whirring orbs on either side that deleted any data they came in contact with. Their cyborg eyes displayed stats on each other and locked onto targets, revealing their exact equations within spacetime. They deployed their tail thrusters and clashed in the virtual eye of a viral hurricane, which slingshotted chunks of decaying, infectious malware that collided with the firewall and disintegrated into oblivion. They blocked and parried each strike steadfastly, resulting in the fight footage mounting to over 900,000 GB of usage. Fortunately, this video must not be narrated here, for it was saved in a zipped folder.

However, one particularly interesting byte featured heinous trash talk exchanged between the warriors. The rebel used his upgraded ~~You-Gee-Oh~~ Luigi-O's (a children's breakfast cereal popular among the only upper class family of four that could afford cereal that featured a mustachioed denim-clad plumber in a green hat and white gloves leaping from behind a large bowl of milk with

Catholic, tasteless wheat-shits and marshmallows shaped like protein-filled mushrooms–angry brown stalks with darker brown shoes–and spicy pasta that grants dragon abilities) arm deck to hack his opponent into the form of a baseball. "Batter up!" he triumphantly jeered as he sent the royalist careening with an oversized baseball bat (Code: 00010011100101001011).

The royalist returned to engage his foe in combat just as quickly as his sharp tongue engaged him in the game of wit. "Hope you saved some of that batter," he forewarned with a swift baton twirl that disarmed his speechless foe, "because I'm about to delete your cookies!" he elaborated as he sublimated the rebel with his staff. The rebel immediately deteriorated into hundreds of pixels, which scattered down into the limitless hells of cyberspace.

The triumphant royalist downloaded the latest smirk sequence from the intergalactic transition portal and allowed the simulation to run its due course as his shadow enveloped the cubic remains of his fallen foe. Yet, unsettlingly, the shadow began to expand, swallowing three, five, twenty corpses, frightening the cowardly light, asserting its aphotic dominance. Behind the royalist roared a hefty chorus of fresh vines snapping and dry roots ripping from their ensconcements, clumps of dirt loosening and raining grungily upon his feet, fat bundles of worms slapping wetly against the ground as their tunnels stretched and lifted and spat them out. One singular degree at a time, the royalist reluctantly forced his head to turn and face what towered behind him. Eyes squinted, facial muscles tensed in anticipation, he gradually lifted his pupils and tilted up his chin to gather the full enormity of the menacing manifestation, and as he took in the facinorous beast, the vividity of triumph vanished from his trembling skin. All of his blood fled in terror to the refuge of his swelling rear-end, leaving his face–where his petrified muscles, flushed with tension that far exceeded their biological limits, all snapped, relaxing in puddles of stringy meat that stretched and rolled pockets of his skin over his eyes and lips– morbidly pallid. For before him creaked the menacing fist of Mother Nature herself, who had finally had enough of man, and who would now enact her unforgiving revenge. The boulders, which had collected into immense, jagged fingers, hurdled down towards the earth, and an avalanche of rock and wood crushed the royalist– who, in his final moments, could barely manage to force his jaw shut as he stared blankly into the raw power of the Earth–into a smelly puddle of shattered bone and scorched blood. As the wave of stones and dust unfolded across the landscape, plastering bodies against the ground, a surge of panic spread through the armies. She had risen.

"She has come! She is here!" they all bellowed, terrified. Screams of death echoed through the night as more fists of rock assembled and smited men into oblivion. Crevices opened up in the Earth, devouring soldiers in plumes of magma and volcanic ash. Ripples of seismic energy rolled across the battlefield, violently displacing pillars of stone as if the ground were a carpet being shaken off in the air. Holes popped open underneath the feet of soldiers, spewing scalding steam into the air at hundreds of miles an hour, instantly melting their flesh and boiling them alive. The clouds heaved bolts of lightning against the armies like raindrops in a spring shower, and the sheer force of their explosive impacts tore limbs from their sockets and heads from spines. Her vengeance was total annihilation—an indignant reminder of the proper hierarchy of the universe: no matter what machines we would build, she was our superior, our creator, our demise, forever, ad infinitum.

I sprinted through the destruction, narrowly dodging mountains plummeting from the sky and skillfully surfing the cresting wave of bubbling lava that drowned the rebels behind me, whose skin popped and bones liquified as the wave slapped against their mutilated faces. After performing a flawless Rodeo-flip while playing an epic guitar solo and kicking Satan in the crotch, I dove from my surfboard (a dead royalist body I had conveniently found) and landed in a flawless split, crushing a maggohound underneath my groin as I did so.

Gathering my reflexes, I remembered that Krüstof had no men fighting alongside him. I gazed at the melting royalist surfboard corpse and realized it was only a maggonoid—a giant humanoid pieced together from millions of maggots to function as a person. It, of course, exemplified merely another one of Krüstof's ridiculous mag-o-failures in laboratory experiments, and it explained the government's constant economic deficiencies; each maggonoid had cost billions to manufacture. A vast reaper-maggot fell upon the corpse, instantly devouring it with its cylindrical coils of canine teeth. It latched onto the maggonoid, writhing and whirligiging until the slapdash meal was thoroughly carboshredded. It thrashed its monumental hind about, slapping flat sides into skulls like deflated basketballs. On the completion of its last resolution, I noticed it had taken my eyes, and I only saw its sights. I looked in the face of death—it was on the front of my head. I tore it off with my hands, which were not to be found. What was real?

The fire spread. It engulfed the bodies of rebels and maggots alike, and my once able-bodied companions reduced to bubbling heaps of molten flesh and soot. Maggots burst from their charred corpses, and cannibalistic, mutated worms feasted on these natural, inferior breeds. I could not find Krüstof, and I paid no mind to the maggots I blindly slaughtered as I searched for the crustacean corpulus. Mag-o-blood spilled loudly as dying maggots and their crust generated a thin film of bloody intestines in and within my hair—both as a whole unit and as individual follicles. A particularly blasphemous maggot latched unto my palm; it met its demise at my rigid forehead. A galactomaggot ultriochomped my neck only to find my xenopomorphic fist an insurmountable obstacle to its existence. A hefty, meat-lubbing maggohound snarled formidably, but one swift wallop on the snout rendered it entirely immobile, for its neck had been dismantled. I galumphed on.

Krüstof had left a trail of putrid slaughter; just as a tornado can be vaguely tracked by its path of destruction—although a tornado could never parallel the maggophile's human devastation— so had been traced the weenieman. Soldiers had been buried alive up to their shoulders, their heads left to be torn apart by the starved maggot hoard. Tongues were excavated from the throat and stapled to rebel foreheads. Serpomaggots slithered into the agape orifices of captured warriors. Corpses leaked thick blood from their bite wounds; several were missing large chunks of their heads or necks, evidently from Krüstof's voracious maw. The list goes on, as did I on my quest.

30: THE ONLY EASY DAY

Captain Coriander, the leader of the Żuk army and a household name in living-room warfare, met my gaze as he resheathed his bloodied sword after wiping the flesh betwixt his furry antennae and polishing his stained eyes by flexing his dangling eye stalks with angsted gusto. A fourteen-meter-tall sasquatchomaggot limpened at his feet as his sword exited its ravaged trachea; its once-mighty bulk served for the remaining beasts' nourishment. Coriander flanked to the left as a screeching ectomaggot chompt the frigid air, which carried such dankness and rotundity that it had to be chewed and swallowed, the round gulps of gas struggling to traverse the capillaries. I pulverized its ghoulish tailbone with a leaping elbow thrust. My weenus successfully punctured its skin and sunk into the wet earth, pinning the beast as Captain Coriander machine-gun-punched its jaw into oblivion.

"Oy, be'ind, yes, !" the unscathed Captain exclaimed, and his warning exhibited promptness enough for me to reach behind my neck and annihilate the gloomphish throat of an attacking dinomaggot. It squirmed annoyingly in my hand, and through forced osmosis it leaked millions of pounds of water into the already soaked atmosphere. Unfortuitously for the beast, this self defense method, devis'd by the Chancellor himself, had never been tested, and Krüstof had overlooked that a maggot was composed of roughly 75-100% water. Therefore, upon liquid eradication, the avaliant creature languished into a sac of blood and veins.

Coriander plunged his sword through the solitary ocular portal of the already razed ectomaggot, and the resultant smoldering shrapnel singed his eyebrows. He punched his blemished face to pop his infectious zits (sadly, he suffered from acute Xenopophrenia, a crippling, terminal infection that results in the volatile eruption of grimy pustules on the brain and scalp– pustules that I habitually took great pleasure in eradicating), and pure, liquid testosterone poured from his trunk as he howled in bloodlust at the death of his foe, clapping his stained hands to shower me in the ectomaggot's baby-blue blood. The beast let out a final sonaric wail as it vaporized into the four-hundredth dimension– from which it had been summoned by Krüstof–and the echolocative soundwave disturbed the forest's maggobats. Yucky was the ichorous sap it left that so successfully defiled my nostrils with its scuzzy fetor.

A sasquatchomaggot's breath massaged my nape, and I jerked my head backwards to meet its maw. It stumbled, and I extended my arm to the ground where Coriander, using his four dexterous limbs, climbed up me so effortlessly that one would think him arboreal. He leapt from my shoulder to kick out the maggot's teeth as I simultaneously hyperextended its fragile knee with a forceful stomp. Coriander savagely reached his hands through the varmint's stomach and sliced them through its flesh randomly in all directions, sending the sasquatchoFAGGOT weeping to its mommy-maggot.

I took hold of Coriander's teensy arm like would have his Żuk brother, and as he held my elbow and fixated his low hanging eyes unto mine, he smirked with his typical battle-loving appetite.

"Le's let 'em 'ave it, oy, I do say! They'll be wishin' they 'ad ne'er mossed wi' us 'ere! Take 'em to Beyond!" He bellowed. Never would walk a braver warrior. Coriander did frighten me, however, for

231

a man who loves the stench of blood cannot be content with peace...

I circled my arm with the attached champion above my head, swinging him with increasing speed in an elliptical orbit about my shoulder. I revolved at deadly G-Force levels, but Coriander only yelped with glee at the immense power his attack would wield. How we did know, I could never decipher, but our minds somehow synchronized, as if our egos had both tapped into the same channel, tuned into one singular frequency bent on mutual hatred for Krüstof, and any thought or idea would be streamed into this void for any other listener to pick up and comprehend.

Finally, we unilaterally released one another's grip, and the Captain rejoiced as he barnstormed the battlefield from above. How beautiful it all was, his thoughts reflected. The glory of battle! The blood, the death, the pandemonium! Order was so stale, so difficult to maintain! How much easier the world would be if disorder and confusion reigned free. And how he enjoyed contributing to the madness, killing mindlessly. Did he truly hate Krüstof, or did he merely love the anarchy of necrosis? No, I considered. The latter could not be possible, for our minds linked in the same channel of thought; I fought because I hated Krüstof, so for us to understand each other, that must also have been his motivation. I wondered what it was that Krüstof had done to Coriander that had so enraged the Captain, for, I knew, Krüstof himself had never ventured into the forest where the Żuk dwelled.

"Full spe'd a'ead! Brace yer maggo-arses!" Coriander hollered. He guffawed in utter delight as his flight speed reached its maximum and his heat capacity nearly exceeded its own limit, for he knew the fireball that engulfed him would shred maggot bodies with mocking ataraxia. And shred it did; billions of maggots met their demise at the hands of the Captain as his conflagrant skull melted their flesh and tore through any resisting tissue. He circled the earth in his flight, and my arm had already latched unto a new trajectory when he passed the battlefield. I caught him midair and seamlessly launched him into a new line of maggots. His body was a flash of light shooting across the sky, utilizing to full advantage the Earth's convenient gravity assist, but the only wish that would come true that night was his own desire for destruction, for the death tolls mounted exponentially at his murd'rous hands.

We were surrounded. The maggot hoard closed in inch by inch, but with each launching of Coriander around the Earth, the organism that was the enemy receded. Entire lines of maggots deliquesced as I threw the Captain, but the gap soon filled with new beasts marching in from the back and sides. On a few occasions, one particularly brave maggot thrust itself forward and broke the stalemate, likely to impress the popular maggots, but in each case Coriander circled back just quickly enough for me to catch him and heave him into the attacker. We screamed in barbarism, overwhelmed by the beauty of battle. So many had died at our hands, and even more at the tendrils of the ever-growing fire. The fire encircled our turf and dismembered the maggot ring, which soon dispatched at the imminent danger; they squirmed directly into the wall of flames, instantly perishing, but choosing to take their chances with the inferno rather than face certain death by continuing to fight Coriander and his Beast. The fire's tentacles licked my ankles, so, sensing my demise neared, I caught Coriander

233

Captain Coriander

as he flew past–this time refraining from release–and his colossal speed propelled us both through the flames and away from the danger. I gazed upon the battlefield and decided I no longer minded the gruesome nature of war. In fact, I considered, the aroma of blood seemed to me actually very pleasing, and almost appetizing...

We landed on the battlefield's outskirts, and I suddenly remembered that I wanted to kill Krüstof. I thanked Coriander for his marvelous service, and we parted ways. Never again would I see that Żuk, for he would die that day in battle, happy as could be.

31: FOR WHOM THE COGS TURN

I finally caught sight of Krüstof after what had been hours of searching through the inner mechanisms of the war machine. Few of my soldiers remained alive, and nearly every Żuk had been slain. Millions of maggot corpses littered the ground, so that each step I took gushed with pus and goo. The only sounds were those of faint screams or the clashing of sword against flesh, coupled with the intensifying roar of the fire. The Chancellor stood nervously a few yards from me, and his sweaty lips quivered as the fire tickled his bottom, for he realized he had no option but to contest me in hand to hand combat.

"This is no place for you! The battlefield. The war!" he snarled.

"I daresay you're afraid. Maggot-boy," I growled.

"You're only a boy! You are! Look how dirty your face is! YOU BOY... YOU STOP!" he scrambled. I sensed his fear. The mighty Chancellor had already been defeated, and our battle had yet to begin.

"How many men did you kill to get to where you are today? How many women? Children?" I demanded.

"What makes you so different? How many have you killed today, and how much did you enjoy their slaughter? Tell me you regret taking their lives! You can't. You and I, we're all too similar. Why conform to what the world considers morally acceptable? What are morals but what a man perceives as acceptable? We are better than our peers! Stronger, smarter! We have the right to rise above them, to take what's ours, to push aside anyone who stands in our way. You and I together could never be stopped. Join me, boy of fire!" nervously pleaded the bargaining crabman, sweat spilling into his mouth and choking his words.

My anger boiled like holy water on the sun, and my veins exploded and flooded my skin with loose, hot blood. What audacity he had, to deem us equals! I deflected his words with an auditory shield. The time had finally come. I screamed in rage, and my rippling muscles bulged out of my skin. I sprinted at Krüstof with outlandish speed. Legends would be told of the battle that ensued, and this is what they would say:

32: Monuments Of Glass/Crab Cakes Are Done!

Krüstof was waddling at top speed when a ground-shaking gigamaggot roar swiped his very arachnidesque foothold from beneath his grotesquely swollen barnacle belly. He gracelessly collapsed into the dusty hellscape like a stick-bug hit with a stun gun, and his knees instantly crunched until his dilapidated kneenises constituted nothing more than a wrinkly bag of crushed chips, but he threw his upper body towards the heavens in a pathetic attempt to continue running. Without the countermovement of his joints, his ankle bones were ground into dust, rendering his lower legs into scrotum-like skin sacs of gleimous blood and pus. The Ghost Boy speedily fell upon the pitiful mollusk cripple like a starving lion warlord upon a blind, deaf, obese, paralyzed, legless deer fetus. He ruthlessly assailed the disgruntled tyrant with several body punches, and Krüstof's bulbous gut was socked so hard that the Ghost Boy's fists collided with the front of his spine, blasting the vertebrae out of his back one by one. The bone shards cascaded over the horizon and ricocheted off of a clan of maggolythic golems and back into Krüstof's skull, penetrating his crusty scalp and lodging themselves in his mushy old crab brain. As the bone shards continued, so did the Ghost Boy's four-hundred-sixty hit combo. It was poor Krüstof's worst nightmare.

Krüstof lost control of his bloodied maw and extended his flat, gray, roast beef tongue due to the nervous severance. The Ghost Boy plummeted his gaseous slug elbow into Krüstof's unprotected jaw. Krüstof's numerous and razor-sharp rotten teeth clamped down on his flimsy tongue. The Chancellor squealed in perfect agony, and for the first time in his life, he prayed, for he knew his soul, ridden with infinite negative karma, was due for chastisement. The Ghost Boy shattered his skull with a brutal right hook, and Krüstof shit his custom eight-legged pants.

The Ghost Boy rotated his shoulders and hit the tyrant with the right so hard that it reversed time. Krüstof unshit the feces, and his skull mended seamlessly. At this point, shaking his claw at the heavens, he concluded that there existed no God. A shrieking dracomaggot swooped down close above the duelers as the Ghost Boy leapt into the air, holding Krüstof by the throat. He shoved the Chancellor's entire belugatine shell into the dracomaggot's unkempt acid anus with one swift motion. He sent his foot in directly after and popped Krüstof out in a makeshift egg of dragon stomach—flawless. Unfortunately for the Chancellor, the ammonia-based digestive acids of the now-stomachless dracomaggot were unbearable.

Krüstof attempted to scamper away on his remaining stumps (only femurs and hips) but failed to cover a yard while entrapped in the biological prison. The Ghost Boy soon returned atop the dracomaggot and flew it directly into Krüstof's egg sac; it burst, expelling maggot feti fragments around the battleground. Scavenger maggots—Krüstof's personal wingèd creations—swarmed upon the fresh jelly and licked the mortal residue clean, and after feverishly devouring the moist appetizer, the ravenous flock picked Krüstof's body apart, leaving only a mangled gut with a wailing head. Krüstof internally howled with black tears streaming from his empty eye sockets. Nearby, a straggling scavenger maggot hacked up the remnants of his soulless seelookers, and Krüstof realized that his

239

previous assumption regarding God was flawed. There indeed reigned a God, he thought, and prowling somewhere within his butchered body rested the hidden corpse of this Almighty Being. But no amount of searching could uncover God's concealed ruins; they lay wedged in a cranny too deep for Krüstof to detect, and they hated him, dooming him to suffer while reminding him bitterly that, if they had wanted to, they could have ended his strife. But worse than the physical damnation inflicted on his mortal vessel was the weenturtling shame that plagued the omnipotent dominator of Grunty Kraba. Defeated by a mere dead child with the body of a slug—how pathetic must he seem to his newfound God!

The Ghost Boy finally finished him off with the ultimate shrekari. He leapt high and glided over Krüstof, whose words besought mercy but whose eyes begged for death. The Ghost Boy extended all of his limbs like a flying squirrel or an angel of death. Directly above Krüstof's head, he contracted all of his muscles impossibly tight, from his core to his throat, and elbowed and kneed Krüstof in the face with all four limbs at once. The Chancellor's head exploded, spraying grey matter and tooth chips into the sky. It instantly replayed in a sick remix, including several alternate angles of the wicked killshot. The repeating squashes of his head could only compare to a baby's plump fist hammering down on a carton of raw eggs, if any earthly being would even dare to mentally replicate the graphic carnage. AHH: the Lives lost!

The Ghost Boy's body caught much of the postmortem splatter, creating a perfect snow angel of absolute victory on the cosmos. The gruesome spritzing blocked by the Ghost Boy lifted his adolescent body into the sky and carried him into the unknown. Our precious hero ascended without a worldly trace, leaving only a cosmic outline of all his grastropodal glory and a burning countryside of warring frankenmaggots. But do cry over his death. Sing about him, for our discord begins now.

33: Crayon Toes, Comatose Toast, Condemned the Most

Krüstof squatted over his ghost's corpse, loudly crackling as he did so. He feared that if rodents did not know of his athletic abilities, they would devour him. He wondered if his name was Matthew. No. But had he asked himself that question? He did not know, because he had never heard anything before. He did know, contrastingly, that he was low on blood, and his feeble supply dwindled every day, hissing in the sun and steaming away. He considered decreasing his body mass to augment his blood:meat ratio. Then he pondered his consideration. He did not know what he thought of that. I did know that he said this before but has not told anyone (1)?

Still as snow in comatose
Whistling winds came slithering through pages
hissing with metal tongues
Fissle, crissle, rissle they rung
Rickety whistle, steely as a blade
Tucked in the thicket of a sullen glade
A cricket tie, tied to wicked lie
tethered like a feather from a tail,

What do we do with such openness? Such a vacuum whose occupancy seems a task too overwhelming for a wounded society to bear... How can the vacancy cease? What can the future hold?

I am sowwy that I wwote this! I did not mean to say this, but, , I do not fink this means somefing. Diswegawd, pwease; I am wwiting nonsense. Owdew has been obwitewated. "Mister[w] Ar[w]igato"? (No, sir; mister can't'nt be spelled that way. I simply won't have it, Not.!) Chaos wesumes.

34: Lamb On The Crossroads

I was not long for that world.

The fire encroached upon me, yet I remained stagnant–I remained for the birds–allowing inaction to corrode my flesh through manifestation as tangible flame. The nether beckoned, whispering sweetly into my bitter ear, unclogging space in its arsenal for my biohazardous being to occupy, for, it knew, I was far too perilous for this Earth.

My legs seemed to be covered in slippery, orange tentacles, and they stung my flesh until it melted. My arms, too, had been blackened by the sooty feelers. They slapped against my calves and clapped against my ankles, feeding, sucking. I knew these serpentine animals would not spare me, but I did not notice them. There were critters inside me…

A chinless man grabbed my face with two hands. His cheeks were tender, warm, old; they squished the sockets in which his eyes no longer resided. His jaw leaked tepid liquid that smothered my lips and neck, and he yelled loudly at me in crazed emotion.

"Larwa! You're on fire! We must–" he yowled polyphonously, multiple voices stringing the same melody, but his remaining words were lost in translation. His eyes were wet and bewildered.

"There are too many critters… I have many critters to deal with. Many young worms…" I confidently but delusionally replied.

"Larwa! Please, don't do this! You've gone mad! There are no worms!"

"I do not see you anymore… the children are too big. They are inside of me. I can feel them, you know. In my stomach. They are long strands… long tubes… around my stomach area. The worms are growing. I've got to get them out," I retorted. The man was crying. But I no longer cared, for some of the orange moving serpents touched him, and he ran away, screaming in pain and calling: "Oh, God! Why have you done this to my poor Larwa?"

There was another man, I think that I thought. On the mountains, I remember. Watching from the mountains. He had no feet. He had a robe, but I could not see his feet; they were under the robe, I think that I thought. White skin, or maybe transparent. Big grin. One arm, only one arm, white skin, big grin, no feet. The air was his vehicle, the wind his throne, the funeral his mother. He was finally real.

I knew the worms flourished in the tubes near my belly. With every second I remained tubular, the Worm Children feti developed further and further, awaiting maximum maturity to make escape possible. I knew they yearned to bore through my sinews... sinews that I cherished far too dearly. The Worm Children had to go, and promptly.

I pulled a feline tooth from my weary, tarrish gums and wiped off the stretchy black gook that stuck to its smooth surface in my stringy hair. I forced the incisor through my chest plate, cleaving my skin, and after one breakneck swipe, my stomach finally saw daylight after years of unfortunate confinement. The warm fog rolled up my chin and billowed into my nose with steamy dankness. I ran my fingers through the scar and peeled my sticky blood apart, and the crackling sound of tendons and nerve connections rattled like the machine-gun fire to which I'd been so accustomed during the war. I tore the two skin sheets off and proceeded to swipe any remaining meat chunks from my ribcage with only a few sloppy

245

handfuls. At last, I thought, my organs could breathe! Moreover, I could eradicate the Worm Children who dwelled within me; there were tubes connected to my stomach… or worms… they had worms in them. No, I thought, they were large mother worms. Yes… they were large worms, and they were pregnant with millions of tiny Worm Children. Yes… I was very comforted that I solved this problem and finally understood what the tubes attached to my stomach bore.

One particularly amorphous organ uncoiled into a clearer, cylindrical shape, and after it revealed a pair of soulless eyes and an unforgivingly parasitic tongue, I remembered that it was in fact another mother tube. No, worm. Unimportant. Whatever it was (I had completely forgotten my realization that the tubes in my gut were in fact gestating worms), I assertively glommed its wrinkled hide and tore it from its roots in my stomach. Warm puddles crawled onto my lap, and I knew this meant I had succeeded in the hellion's assassination. How red my hands were–but this I also knew to be normal and good. The worm had been ousted, and for this I rejoiced.

BUT SOFT. Methinks I did detect further wormage! OoOo (DIE WORMS).

The other BLOBS stupidly became worms before my eyes. ThEiR Loss. Wormbeing entails a dreary existence indeed. If I knew I already wormwas in the past my wormind could never comprehend being awormianly. Best not to ponder on these matters. What was I to do? If they chose to wormbe over the carefree life of a useless shape, So It Would Be. The panicked sniffles and snorts from their soft slimy snouts were amply-fied exponentially by my adrenaline-inducing paranoia. I do not think they liked me there.

THE WORMS DESCENDED TO THEIR PROPER HABITAT OF THE INFERNO. I gladly severed their internal connections with my dumb body. Good riddance, Worm Children.

Suddenly, a hunger of fantastic proportions overtook my thoughts and rusted my mental gears shut. The worms I'd slaughtered appeared unsettlingly appetizing, and I indulged myself in their fats. My feet followed, though I failed to notice. It was not long before my exposed stomach accommodated both my legs, the many Worm Children, and my pelvis. The warm liquids continued to spill, and I sponged clots of the bright wetness with my remaining skin so that my muscles and bones were held together only by a thick, weak, scarlet cloth instead of living epidermis. My ears dripped cruor amply and therefore drowned out auxiliary disquietude, so I neglected the fire's deafening reverberation.

I desperately yearned to recapture my misguided consciousness, but it was far too tightly wedged betwixt—nay, intwixt; yes, better—the crevices of insanity for recovery. I ached excruciatingly, and my vision was obscured by scorched earth and charred blood. My eyes sweated and bled; they became overtaken by the inferno. I allowed my body to roast in successful celebration, for I knew I had done well.

Fathers, brothers, friends, we have not died in vain.

35: A Snipped String Lies Limp

I strolled a grassy pass that would eventually end its path in the side of the mountain, where it collided with and rebounded off of the slab of grey into the sky. The mountain stretched to great heights, scratching the bottom of the man on the moon. As it reached above the clouds like an outstretched arm, the dense layer of pines dissolved up the slope and became ever sparse. Unable to travel the treacherous vertical path, I turned my attention to the forking walkways that straddled the mountain. I traversed the flowery trail to face the two distant forest entities. To my left: a thick cherry rosewood realm. To my right: a lusher and leafier oak timberland on which I focused.

Out of the provinces of this dextral country, a curdled troll man emerged from the eaves, transgressing hotly beneath the overhanging canopy. He tore through the bush, and I halted in fascination. I crouched, and my knees ached from the waning pains of death, but I was adamant to observe the trifling boreal beast. Impressed by my own ability to conceal my human presence, I studied the droll man as if I'd been entitled to. The earth-dolven faggot gangrelled as he pressed on through the bramble that confined the woodlands like a spined girdle. He attempted to demonstrate a mobile finesse that he did not possess; he stumbled often in an amateur attempt to evade the forest's low-hanging fruits and obstructing vines. Ahead, the troll dove through the net of thorn and gracelessly thudded onto the path's clearing. He jogged forward to what perhaps seemed to be a concealed troll encampment, but made no enter. He pivoted to face me, folded his arms across his broad chest, and then glared through me. I'd been speckledorfed; I realized I had not been observing in secret, but, rather, he had monitored me and deliberately crossed our paths in inevitable confrontation.

I approached acquiescently. This was no troll, but a hallucination of some sorts. An odd entity of varying color perched itself upon an ethereal floating stool. His magical vehicle, the golden Chúfa pepper, sparkled with searing white lights like those of the sun, gently cascading stellar dust which inexplicably failed to accumulate upon the ground. The immobile blob of slime and untethered fat viscously exhibited a show of intricate patterns and colors as he flashed chromatophorically like an intoxicated chameleon. His skull, the only appendage to his vessel, twisted towards me as swollen skin flaps cushioned the delicately circumscribed face within. His brows gestured to the thick of the vegetation; long mushrooms sprouted with fluorescent domes, bending like crooked palms; rich, summer-green grasses edged the pathway into the infinite vines; my arm collected the cascading honeysuckles and drew them apart like curtains from a window. I stared into the dormant tunnel, observing the visible silence echo within—a cubic, structured silence with a shiny texture and visible weight that tired the ears as they attempted to listen and pained the mind in a blur of audible confusion. I turned once more to the peculiar floating figure.

He nodded, then instructed me to "take of the Chúfa pepper" in a strangely inhuman voice, one too round and perfect to take origin in our flawed race, and one that lacked an epicenter, resonating equally from all points in the ambient space. He gorged the succulent pepper with the aid of newly sprouted hands, groping

249

at the pulp as it gloshed internally. Saps rolled off his forearm, and he hurled a portion of the pepper into my awaiting maw. I chewed at the bitter pepper, and it became intensely delectable. Afterwards, he nodded thrice more to the cave, silently coercing me to inspect it one more time. Unfortunately, these nods proved too vigorous for his neck, which snapped embarrassingly. I turned my back as he wailed, and my cheeks reddened as the awkwardness rose. The screams finally ceased after a moment's shame, and when I turned back to him, he smiled again as if nothing had occurred.

I peered past the honeysuckles again, noting the meanders of the cavernous sanctuary. I felt the Chúfa pepper melt inside my stomach, releasing a warm, liquid comfort. Suddenly, within the quakes of a spontaneous pulse of dimensional fury, the perception of depth within the confines of the mountain's cavity became nonexistent, and the tunnel folded like a wizard's accordion.

The space into which I stared—a two-dimensional barrier composed of infinite expansion—howled at me darkly. Wisps of energy leapt from the horizontal pane like spirit coys from the surface of a glass lake and swirled around me, gently tugging me, requesting my entry. My eyes grazed the surroundings, combing for an explanation. What was the destination of my Chúfa-induced euphoric trave? The writings assimilate into the folds of my brain without visual interpretation.

My exocranial existence zrozeephed and expired, and white noise grated my eardrums as boisterous sirens and thousands of maximum-voltage electrical discharges reigned supreme in my remaining essence. I knew all too well where to travel next, though I'd never been explicitly told; instead, a silent yet resounding voice summoned me from a nearby cave. The commander of this insistent utterance heavily implied his name to be Oświec, and somehow he insinuated his most prolific title to be the Protector of Universal Truth, among many others.

The blackness and nothingness I'd been observing inside the tunnel suddenly gave way to sprouting mushrooms, along with other fungi, and instantly I became certain—not individually, but certain in a sense of textbook truth—that the creation of this Mushland, as I came to call it, was entirely Oświec's doing. I attempted to feel one of the many 'shrooms' porous surfaces, but, unfortunately, they existed in a two-dimensional world, and my round, grubby fingers only intersected with it on one plane, causing an unexpectedly excruciating wave of slicing pain as my fingertips were cleanly cleaved off my hand and sparks of violet energy rained into the atmosphere. As I approached the cave in which the omniscient Oświec reigned, the two-dimensionality of the swamplands behind me gradually receded; the dimension-coefficient descended through various inexistent decimals before finally screeching to a sudden halt at zero-D. The interior of the cave, however, mysteriously remained invisible, glowing with a shade of colorlessness that somehow failed to resemble blackness but could not be recognized by an unenlightened mind. Oświec "stood" ominously by my side, making his presence known while, of course, refraining from physically manifesting himself, and he coaxed me to step into the void, for he sensed my confusion. I did not refuse his command.

The disintegration of one's body is a curious endeavor. As my fleshy spirit transversed the rift into the cave's salivating mouth, zero-dimensionality warmly enveloped my once extant chassis. I dissolved into oblivion, and the process was surprisingly painless and spiritually satisfying. Zero-D exist-d'AUNce was not, popular to contrary belief, empty. Instead, all my surroundings felt strangely full and solid, though I found movement through them exotically fluid, and they glowed with hues inconceivable by human eyes–colors with depth and thickness, with sound, texture, weight. When I attempted to look back to the so different world of dimensionality, the portal had vanished, and it became clear that the Keeper's lair would be my place of residence for a substantial spell.

Oświec continued to deny me the pleasure of looking upon his insightful face; indeed, only one discernible pattern emerged in the entire dimension: a toppled sign slanted on a slouched, floating mound, bearing text written in every language, many of which, I assumed, originated on other planets or planes of existence. "Welcome to the Zero Zone; Population: Unknown" the sign ambiguously declared…

EPILOGUE

Larwa Chłopak's smudge on the manuscript of history soon faded into oblivion. Word of the rebellion reached the Siberian Overlords seven months after Krüstof's death, thanks to the newly reinvented electrical telegraph (although, unfortunately, an inventor daring enough to redevelop wire after the Reverse Industrial Revolution had yet to arrive, meaning one telegraph pole had to be manually hoisted to the next to transmit messages upon a tap of the tips of the poles). The Soviets promptly issued a replacement Chancellor of Punishment, and he made quick work of exterminating remaining opposition among the Gruntian masses. The spirit of liberty so thoroughly championed by Larwa's followers was easily forgotten by the porridge-minded slobs of Grunty Kraba, and the beauty of anarchy tragically vanished. Order resumes, and what a pity it is.

Oh, what a pity it is…

NOTES:

WRITE YOUR OWN CHAPTER (YOU HAVE TO):

Made in the USA
Columbia, SC
01 September 2017